THE SECRET PEOPLE

John Wyndham was born in 1903. Until 1911 he lived in Edgbaston, Birmingham, and then in many parts of England. After a wide experience of the English preparatory school he was at Bedales from 1918 to 1921. Careers he tried included farming, law, commercial art, and advertising, and he first started writing short stories, intended for sale, in 1925. From 1930 to 1939 he wrote stories of various kinds under different names, almost exclusively for American science fiction publications. He also wrote detective novels. During the war he was in the Civil Service and afterwards in the Army. In 1946 he went back to writing. His most famous novels are THE DAY OF THE TRIFFIDS, THE KRAKEN WAKES (both of which have been translated into several languages), THE MIDWICH CUCKOOS (filmed as THE VILLAGE OF THE DAMNED) and TROUBLE WITH LICHEN. John Wyndam died in 1969.

Also by the same author, and available in Coronet Books:

Stowaway to Mars
Wanderers of Time
Sleepers of Mars

The Secret People

John Wyndham

writing as JOHN BEYNON

CORONET BOOKS
Hodder and Stoughton

First published in Great Britain by
George Newnes, Ltd., London

Coronet Edition 1972
Eighth impression 1977

The characters and situations in this book are entirely imaginary and bear no relation to any rea person or actual happening

Printed and bound in Great Britain for
Hodder and Stoughton Paperbacks, a
division of Hodder and Stoughton Ltd.,
Mill Road, Dunton Green, Sevenoaks,
Kent (Editorial Office: 47 Bedford
Square, London, WC1 3DP)
by Richard Clay (The Chaucer Press) Ltd,
Bungay Suffolk

ISBN 0 340 15834 4

THE SECRET PEOPLE

Unlike few other English writers of science-fantasy who were obliged to turn to America for their early encouragement, John Beynon was fortunate to taste a fair measure of success in his own country before the war interrupted his efforts. It was in 1935 that his first full-length novel was serialised in Odham's *Passing Show*, a family weekly lavishly designed on the lines of America's *Saturday Evening Post*. This had started off by making great play with American science fiction of more universal appeal, including Edgar Rice Burrough's tales of John Carson's exploits on Venus; and the periodical offered an appropriate billet for *The Secret People*. It proved so popular that it was soon followed by Beynon's *Stowaway to Mars*, which has an equally honoured place in the annals of British science fiction.

The Secret People is set in the 1960s; and though the rocket plane which seemed a reasonable possibility in 1935 was pushed off the drawing board by the jet, the motive power of the rocket has enabled us to reach far beyond the stratosphere into outer space – an achievement which then seemed utterly fanciful. And if the New Sea has not yet materialised, we have heard enough in recent years of the drowning of African villages and the painstaking shifting of ancient Nubian monuments in the interests of vast irrigation projects involving millions of acres of land. As for the pygmies who inhabit the cavern world beneath the desert, there is no record of their existence beyond the realm of the author's fertile imagination. But the Dark Continent has not yielded all her secrets; and by the time you reach the end of this story you may well find yourself believing in *The Secret People* . . . even haunted by them, as their creator was haunted for years by the memory of the Morlocks after reading, in his schooldays, Wells' immortal tale of *The Time Machine*.

WALTER GILLINGS

PART I

CHAPTER I

ON an afternoon in September 1964, the ears of the inhabitants of Algiers were unpleasantly assaulted by an uproar from the skies. The sound was different from the familiar drumming boom of the regular mail and passenger service, and it was equally unlike the staccato throbbing of the desert police patrols; it was, in fact, an entirely new brand of aerial noise, more offensive than either. The strollers in the streets stopped to look up, the loiterers in cafés moved from under their striped awnings, even the hagglers in the markets momentarily suspended business to stare surprisedly overhead.

The cause of the sensation came streaking across the blue Mediterranean—a small silver aeroplane, hurling itself out of the northern sky. It amazed the watchers that so small a craft could make so fierce a noise, but the sight of it astonished them no less, for it roared through the heavens, trailing behind it a wake of flame fully six times its own length. It was diving as it crossed the city, coming down to earth like a silver comet with a scarlet tail. A moment later it had passed out of sight. The crackling roar of its engines grew less and presently ceased. Algiers, with a few caustic censuals of the noise-loving pilot, turned back to its business and its drinks, and forgot the silver plane's existence.

Mark Sunnet taxied the plane to a stop and emerged from his cabin to greet the astonished aerodrome authorities. He was polite to them, but not expansive. He had grown weary of the sensation which inevitably attended his arrivals and departures, and frequent explanations to interested authorities of the superiority of his machine over the ordinary propeller-driven craft had become tedious. Accordingly, he pleaded tiredness. He had flown, he told them, non-stop from Paris, and proposed spending only one night in Algiers before pushing on to the south. Could anyone, he added, recommend him to a comfortable hotel? A member of the aerodrome staff suggested that the Hôtel de Londres could provide hot baths, comfortable beds, and excellent food. He thanked the man, gave instructions for the care of his plane, and, leaving it still surrounded by a crowd of inquisitive pilots and ground staff, made his way to the Customs Office. Emerging a few minutes later with his papers stamped and in order, he hailed a taxi.

'I want to go to the Hôtel de Londres,' he said.

The driver expressed surprise in a theatrical manner.

'The Hôtel de Londres, monsieur?' he inquired doubtfully.

'Certainly,' said Mark. 'What's wrong with that?'

'Alors, monsieur. It is a good hotel, no doubt, but not of the best. It is bourgeois. Monsieur has not the bourgeois air, that is evident. He should honour the Hôtel de l'Etoile, there is not a doubt of it. It is a house of the most magnificent, it is modern, it is——'

'All right. Let's have a look at it.' Mark cut the eulogy short by climbing into the cab.

Fate is not above using inconsiderable details for her obscure purpose. Thus, the whole of Mark's future was destined to depend on the trifling fact that an Algerian taxi-driver was brother to the head waiter in a hotel.

Five days later found him, still a guest of the Hôtel de l'Etoile, lounging at ease upon its broad balcony. He lay with his head turned at an angle which enabled him to watch the occupant of the next chair. The busy harbour of Algiers, lively and brilliant in the sunshine, backed by the deep blue of the Mediterranean was a panorama which could wait: for the present, Margaret claimed all his attention. He half hoped that she would not wake to disturb his placid comfort.

It was a long time since he had been allowed to indulge in the luxury of complete laziness. Of the last six years, business had occupied almost every waking hour. He had devoted himself doggedly to the uninspiring task of propping up a tottering shoe business which only the timely death of an unprogressive uncle had saved from complete disaster. The firm of Sunnet had been established over a century and had retained in the trade a reputation for turning out good, reliable stuff. And that, the uncle, an inveterate recliner upon laurels, had considered to be good enough.

The prospects of salvaging the hopelessly old-fashioned firm had been slender when Mark inherited. Almost without exception his advisers had been for selling to cut his losses, but Mark had developed a streak of obstinacy which surprised himself. He had found himself looking at the rocky business of Sunnet's not merely as a means of livelihood, but as a challenge, and he went to work as much in a spirit of bravado as from hope of gain.

He had not been brilliant, but he had shown an obstinate determination to overcome prejudice against the firm. Gradually the trade became aware that Sunnet's was no longer a back number; their shoes were once more being demanded and worn by the million, and Mark emerged from the cocoon of work which he had spun about him to find himself not only vindicated, but a man of means. And this was the time to slack off. He had no intention of devoting his life to shoes, nor to the making of money from shoes. He had done what he had set out to do, and with the concern forging ahead, he felt the need of personal freedom. He had called his managers together and told them that he intended to go away for a while.

'Finding new markets, sir?' the chief buyer inquired hopefully.

'God forbid. I'm going to have a holiday—a real holiday. And I'm not leaving an address. It'll be up to you fellows to manage things between you while I'm away.'

His first step had been to buy a machine lately imported from America. The makers, unromantic men of little imagination, had been able to find no better name for their product than 'Strato-Plane'. Mark, after one flight in it to those regions far above the clouds, renamed it the *Sun Bird*; and the *Sun Bird* it remained.

The first three weeks of his new leisure he occupied in trans-European flitting. Paris, Copenhagen, Stockholm, Warsaw, Berlin, Vienna, Paris again; hither and thither with all the delight of a child in a new toy until he tired of fast movement for its own sake and began to contemplate a less hurried, though more extensive, trip. The *Sun Bird*'s flying range was immense and the world lay open to him. There was little sense in restricting himself to

Europe where one large city was, after all, not very unlike another, when he had the time and the means to range as far as he wished. Moreover, he found himself growing a trifle tired of his own exclusive society. Accordingly, he had bethought him of a friend now farming in Cape Province, and the *Sun Bird* was turned to the south.

But now his intended trip had been cut short before it had well begun. His proposed stop of one night in Algiers had already been multiplied by five, and looked like extending still more. And the reason for his change of plan was reposing in the chair beside him.

Her head lay back on its deep red curls against a cushion, and her slender, sun-browned hands rested, fingers interlocked, in her lap. Her face, too, had acquired a tinge of golden brown and the African sun had raised upon it the faintest scatter of shadows—scarcely dark enough to be called freckles. Mark approved critically. Many of the red-haired girls he had known, he reflected, had had an unsatisfactory, a kind of unfinished look about the eyes, but there was no trace of that in Margaret's face. The hazel eyes themselves were hidden now behind lids trimmed with perfectly genuine dark lashes. Her mouth, not too large, but certainly without any petulant smallness, was curved in a slight smile. The smile increased as he watched. The lids lifted.

'Well, do you approve of it?'

Mark laughed. 'I thought you were asleep.'

'Most women know when they are being inspected.'

'Then you can never really sleep in public.'

'Thank you, sir.'

She smiled at him again and stretched her arms lazily. Mark swung his legs to the floor and sat up, looking out into the hot sunshine across the shimmering water. Both of them felt that it was time to make a move, but the day did not encourage activity.

'What shall we do?' he asked her.

'I don't know. You suggest something.'

Mark reflected. The tennis courts were not far away, but they would be simmering like hot-plates on such a day. There was the swimming pool; or they might go a little way up the coast and bathe, or . . .

'What about the New Sea? We've neither of us seen

that yet.'

She turned, surprised.

'But it's ever so far from here—right beyond the mountains. Three or four hundred miles. Even in a plane——'

'In an ordinary plane it would take some time,' he agreed, 'but not in my *Sun Bird*. You wait till I show you. It's just an afternoon jaunt for a rocket plane.'

'A rocket plane? Like the new American mail carriers?'

'Well, hardly as big as all that, but she *is* a rocket plane. There aren't many of them about yet, but there will be soon: they're the coming thing, not a doubt of it.'

The girl looked doubtful.

'But are they quite safe?'

'The *Sun Bird*'s taken me safely enough all round the continent and brought me across here. Besides, do you think I'd suggest your going in her if she weren't the safest thing in the skies? You wait till you see her. Hurry up and change, then I'll show you.'

Margaret Lawn made her way obediently towards the lift. The business of changing she performed almost automatically, using her mirror with an unwonted perfunctoriness. Her holiday was progressing in an expected and yet in an unexpected manner. Mark, for instance, had not been entirely unexpected—not that she had ever seen or even heard of him before, but the occasion was bound to provide a playmate of some kind. He might have been called Tom or Dick or Harry: he happened to be called Mark. Nevertheless, the state of affairs at present was not quite as she had foreseen. Events were not proceeding quite according to the course plotted for them. She had a sensation as though she were trying to steer a car with a wheel which had too much play. One got along without accidents, but there was an unwonted breathlessness, an unusual lack of assurance. More disturbing she found the growing conviction that she did not want to steer, and that it no longer amused her to apply the manoeuvring skill which she had displayed on previous occasions. This was the more irritating in that there was nothing striking about Mark to account for it. He was really a perfectly ordinary young man, and Margaret, like many another, had not felt that she was destined to fall in love with an ordinary young man. And yet it was happening—had happened. She was irritable with herself. She, Margaret Lawn, who had hitherto with justification considered herself reliable, capable, and a mistress of difficult situations, was undergoing an unwilling change; realising, with feeble protest, that she quite incredibly *wanted* to hand over the controls. Changing, full in the face of all her principles, from an active to a passive: and, worse still, half enjoying the change.

It did not take her long to slip off her light frock and put on more serviceable clothes. In general—that is, apart from present emotional uncertainties—she was a young woman who knew her own mind and disdained the more elementary tricks. Her reappearance on the balcony was made with little delay.

'Will it do?' she asked.

Mark rose from his chair and looked at her neat white riding suit with approval.

'My dear, it couldn't be better. Even if it wouldn't do, it suits you far too well for me to say so.'

They took a taxi to the aerodrome where Mark's orders for his machine to be wheeled out set the mechanics bustling.

Rocket-propelled planes were still such a novelty that his was the first to be seen in Algiers. A few were in experimental service upon the mail routes, but the general public knew them only from photographs. A privately owned stratosphere rocket was all but unique upon the eastern side of the Atlantic, and as she was drawn clear of the hangar most of the ground staff within sight hurried to lend interested assistance.

'And that's your *Sun Bird*?' Margaret said, watching the attendants trundle the little plane into the sunlight.

Mark nodded. 'How do you like her? Looks a bit quaint at first sight, I'll admit.'

'I think she's lovely,' the girl answered, without moving her gaze from the glittering silver shape.

The *Sun Bird*'s proportions differed noticeably from those of propeller-driven aircraft. Her fuselage was wider and decidedly shorter, and the wings stubbier and broader. Two windows were set right in the nose and others well forward in the sides. Despite the unfamiliar shape caused chiefly by new problems of weight distribution, there was no effect of squatness: she looked what she was, a compact little bundle of power, as different from the ordinary plane as a bumble bee from a seagull.

Mark made a short investigation—somehow he never managed to feel as easy about foreign mechanics as he did about the home variety—but he found no cause for complaint. The fuel tanks were full and all the necessary adjustments had been faithfully made. He unlocked the cabin door and slid into the driving seat, beckoning the girl in beside him. She followed and looked round with interest. The two seats were set side by side right in the nose. In the small cabin was room for more seats behind them, but either these had never been fixed, or Mark had had them removed. Against the sides was a series of lockers and cupboards, and to metal staples set in the floor and walls were attached straps for the purpose of securing any loose baggage.

Mark was shouting final instructions to the ground staff, warning them to stand well clear unless they wished to be grilled. Then he slammed the door, cutting off all sound from the outer world. He advised Margaret to lean her head against the padded rest behind her seat.

'The acceleration's a bit fierce when we take off,' he explained.

She leaned back obediently, and he looked out of the window to make certain that the men had taken his advice to heart.

'Right. Here we go then.'

He gripped the stick with one hand, and with the other advanced a small lever set in the left arm of his seat. A roaring drone broke out: a cluster of fiery daggers stabbed from the bunch of rocket ports in the tail. The whole sturdy little ship shuddered and jumped. Then she was off, hurtling across the field, spitting flames behind her. Margaret felt as if a great invisible weight were pressing her back into her seat.

Suddenly the *Sun Bird* seemed to leap from the ground. Nose up, she soared, climbing into the blue African sky at an angle which caused the watching ground staff's jaws to drop. For a few minutes she was visible as a glitter of steel and a flash of fire in the heavens, then she was gone, leaving only a trail of smoke to show her path.

The chief mechanic shook his head; the *Sun Bird* struck him as being a bit too new-fangled, he felt no temptation to ride on a roaring rocket. His comrades were agreeing among themselves that her climb was *magnifique*, but that the din of her discharge was *épouvantable*.

Mark flattened out at twenty-one thousand feet and turned the nose to the south-east. He smiled at the girl.

'Like it?'

'It certainly is the last word in lifts, but I'm not quite sure that I really like it. I'm not frightened, but—well, it is a bit breath-taking at first, isn't it?'

'You soon get used to that.'

They had to raise their voices only slightly, for the makers had lined the hull with an efficient sound-deadening material, and the windows consisted of double sheets of non-splintering glass with a semi-vacuum between. The result was to reduce the roar of the rocket discharges to no more than a constant, muffled drone.

'Look down there,' Mark said.

A view of the North African coast bordering the vivid Mediterranean was spread for them. At such a height no movement was visible. Land and sea were laid out in the sunlight, looking oddly artificial; like a vast, brilliantly coloured relief map beneath a huge arc light. The blue was cut off sharply by the green of the coast, which gave way gradually to the darker hues of the mountains to the south. To Margaret's unaccustomed eyes the plane was suspended almost stationary above an untrue world.

'Are we moving at all?' she asked.

For answer, Mark pointed to the speed indicator. The needle was hovering around the two-hundred mark, and she could see that it was slowly making its way higher.

'It's the height,' he explained. 'If there were any clouds about, you'd realise our speed. As it is, you can't, but you should be getting your first glimpse of the New Sea within the hour.'

The tall peaks of the Tell Atlas rose before them and Mark sent the *Sun Bird* soaring higher still. The speed increased as the resistance of the thin atmosphere outside grew less. He glanced at another instrument for assurance that the air supply was maintaining correct pressure within.

The mighty range of mountains now looked like a badly crumpled cloth far below. Before long the broad Plateau of the Shotts slid into view, the lakes upon it glittering like pieces of broken mirror casually dropped among the mountains. Beyond, on the starboard bow, sprawled the final spurs of the great Atlas range, the Saharan Atlas, the walls of the desert, where they ended stood the ancient town of Biskra, still guarding, as it had for untold centuries, the pass to the north. Mark changed his course a few points east. And then, as they cleared a range of lesser mountains, came their first view of the latest wonder of the world, the New Sea.

The idea of the New Sea was not in itself new. Back in the nineteenth century the great De Lesseps—previous to his entanglements over the projected Suez Canal—had started his countrymen toying with the New Sea scheme much in the same way as the English played with the idea of a Channel Tunnel. Then, after being for almost a century a matter of merely academic interest it had, in 1955, suddenly become practical politics. The French, in fact, decided to flood a part of the Sahara Desert.

That the undertaking was within the range of possibility had long been admitted by many experts, but until France had discovered Italy's willingness to enter into partnership, the financial obstacles had proved insurmountable. Through mutual assistance and for their mutual benefit the two nations had gone to work upon the most ambitious engineering scheme yet projected.

Nature has chosen to frown upon many parts of the world, but in few places has she glowered more fiercely than in North Africa, and it would seem likely that the centre of her disapproval in that region was Tripolitania. There would be difficulty in finding an equal-sized piece of land with a better claim to the title of world's worst colony. There was little more than a strip of fertile coast closely backed by the most hopeless of deserts, but for all that the Italians, for reasons of pride and prestige, had clung to it with a magnificent obstinacy. And now the French scheme offered them the opportunity of turning a liability into an asset.

France could foresee in the creation of this inland sea several advantages for herself. First, she hoped that southern Tunis and a part of Algeria would benefit. The New Sea was to be begun by merging the Tunisian lakes—or 'Shotts'—which were already below sea level. It was argued that the land about it would rapidly become fertile. Trees would grow, clouds would follow, bringing rain; the rain would induce still more vegetation, and so on until the erstwhile desert sands should bloom. Moreover, Tripolitania, lying on one shore of the sea, would also benefit, thus she would be enabled to support colonists from Italy and so lessen the dangerous condition of overpopulation on the other side of the Alps. Italy, once satisfied that there was no catch in the plan, became equally enthusiastic. If her barren property should become fertile, at least in part, colonial expansion would give her a chance to build up a yet larger population. The great day when the might of the Roman Empire should be revived would be brought a step nearer.

The conferences between the two nations were remarkable both for their rapidity in making decisions and for their lack of discord. Early in 1956 the work was put in hand, and the enterprise was pushed forward with such determination and success that in March 1962, water began to gush from the first of the great pipes into the sandy waste.

Now, in September 1964, the lakes, large and small, were already merged. Seen from the air, one great shining sheet of water stretched out of view to the east and to the south. Here, in the north-west corner, the sea would not extend a great deal farther. Already it was lapping at the lower slopes of the foothills, and though its level would rise, its advance would be small. The new coast was dotted with patches of high ground still above the flood level; temporary islands soon to be submerged. Over the lower parts the water had already risen until only bunches of green palm heads broke the surface, looking like beds of reeds.

Mark put the *Sun Bird* into a dive and they crossed the water's edge close to an Arab village of white, flat-roofed houses. It had stood upon a slight knoll, but already the water was creeping in through the doors of the highest dwellings, while the lower could be seen, still standing, beneath the surface. They would not last long, he reflected. Built as they were, for the most part, of baked mud, they would soon revert, crumbling and sliming away to leave no sign save a few stones. There was something desolate and unhappy about this village, condemned after centuries of sunny existence to a watery dissolution. A faint sense of depression touched the two in the plane.

'It makes everything seem so impermanent,' Margaret thought aloud. 'It's like destroying a piece of history. I know it's silly and sentimental to feel like that, but I do. For hundreds of years people have lived and fought here—camel caravans have plodded across these sands; and now they'll never do it again.' She paused, and then added: 'It's the irrevocability of it, I suppose. There's always something sad—and rather frightening—when one thinks of things as irrevocable.'

Mark caught her mood and agreed with it.

'Yes. There will be new towns of flat, white houses by the new shores. They'll look the same, perhaps, but they won't be the same. The air of changelessness will have gone for good—you can't inject history. It's a funny thing that we always see the past through rose-coloured glasses, unless we really set out to get at the truth.... I mean, that village was undoubtedly squalid, life was hard in it and probably cruel, yet one regrets its passing. A queer streak of conservatism we've all got.'

He drove the plane still lower, passing over a grove of palms which bore their dates though the trunks were now awash. Children had climbed the trees to gather the last harvest they would yield, dropping the fruit down into crude boats moored below. They looked up and waved to the plane as it passed.

The two flew on for some minutes without speaking. The New Sea stretched beneath them to the horizon now in every direction, save the north. Mark pointed to the mountains which held it back.

'One day they'll build a pleasure city on those slopes, and all Europe will come here to bask in the sun and swim in the sea. I shall be there. And you?'

She considered, smiling slightly.

'It may be a long time to wait. Suppose I get old and ugly before they've built their city?'

'My dear, don't be blasphemous. There are still some impossibilities even in this world. Older you must certainly get, but ugly ... Margaret, if you should live to be a hundred, it couldn't happen ...'

At its eastern end the sea ran back in a narrow arm towards the source. Before long the *Sun Bird* came within sight of the twelve vast pipes which fed it. For two and a half years now they had been at their work of pouring foaming, man-made cataracts into the desert. Day and night the stupendous pumps, twenty miles away in Qabés, had sucked up their millions of gallons to send them churning and swirling along the pipes. But huge as the conduits were, it remained unbelievable that they alone could be the instruments for submerging all these square miles of land; that it was only water passed by them which was lapping ever higher and farther across the sands. The loss by evaporation alone, Mark considered, must be immense in this region. There was no day during which the sun did not broil down with full intensity to draw up its tons of moisture. From the beginning there had been sceptics who had looked on the plan as a fantasy, and he felt bound to admit that had he seen this place before the start of operations, he would have been one of them. The immensity of the task was stupefying; yet it was succeeding in a way which caused the engineering triumphs of Panama and Suez to dwindle into insignificance. Whether the ultimate results would justify its sponsors remained yet to be seen.

They passed over the gushing outlets, following the twelve-fold pipe-line across higher country, and it was a matter of only a few minutes before Qabés came into view. Both of them were somewhat prepared for the sight by the photographs which had appeared in every illustrated paper, but the scale of operations took them by surprise. It had been necessary not only to build enormous housings for the pumps and gear, but to alter the town itself. It was no longer an Arab town which lay beside the Gulf of Qabés. Smoke, noise, and fuss reeked up to insult the African sky from a city which might have been transported bodily from one of the less pleasant industrial districts of Europe. If ever a place deserved to be called a blot on the fair face of nature, it was the transformed town of Qabés.

But one had to admit that a job was being done, and done well; it was to be hoped that the end would justify all this filth and furor which was the means. Head-cloth had been ousted by cloth cap, tractors and cars had supplanted camel and donkey, the blue sea was polluted with waste oil, the palms bore sooty dates among sooty fronds. And yet the pumps were a triumph, a glory of power.

Mark had a hankering to inspect them. One day, he decided, he would come over here and examine the works at his leisure. For the present ... He looked inquiringly at Margaret. She pulled a face of distaste. He knew that she was seeing nothing beyond the dirt and destruction. She did not catch the feeling of strength and triumph over nature which lay behind it all.

'All right, we'll leave it now,' he said. 'We can go back again over the New Sea if you like—or we might keep round by the Mediterranean coast and have a look at Rome's old sparring partner, Carthage.'

Margaret shook her head at the alternative.

'The New Sea, I think. This place has shocked me, and one shock is enough for the day. If they've treated Carthage anything like they've treated Qabés, then *delenda est Carthago* indeed.'

Mark circled the plane and set off back over the pipelines. He held the same course until the sea was reached, when he altered a few points to the south of their outward journey. They drew clear of the old borders of the Shott el Jerid and found the newly inundated land where numerous islets varying in nature and extent from a few square yards of sand to well planted groves of trees still survived. They descended until they were scudding a bare hundred feet above the water, able to look down on the strange sight of palms masquerading as marine growths.

'There's another village,' Margaret pointed out. 'But this one's breaking up: all the roofs have gone already, and some of the walls. I'm glad. It would be too eerie to think of fish making their homes where people once lived, swimming along the streets, and in and out of the windows and doors....'

Mark laughed. The notion struck him as delightfully absurd. He had started to reply when a sudden tremendous explosion cut him short.

The *Sun Bird* careered wildly, flinging both of them out of their seats. For a moment she seemed to stand on her tail; then, slipping and twisting, she plunged towards the water....

CHAPTER II

MARK opened his eyes and shut them again quickly. The glare of a brilliant shaft of sunshine through the window felt like a white hot wire in his head. The pulsing aches inside it magnified themselves a hundred times. After a short pause he wriggled slightly into the shadow and reopened his eyes more cautiously. This time he was successful in keeping them open. Shots of pain tore through his head, but, with the help of agonised facial contortions, it was possible to bear them. For an idle minute he lay regarding the roof of the *Sun Bird* uncomprehendingly until the memory of events jumped back at him. He shrugged to a sitting position and held his head in his hands. When the throbbing had eased a little he ventured to look round. The *Sun Bird* was on an even keel; a slight rise and fall told him that she was afloat.

'Margaret!' he called suddenly.

She lay crumpled beside him. The red curls spreading tangled on the floor hid her face. But there was an abandon about her whole pose which acted on him like a physical shock. He turned her over gently to find her face almost as white as the suit she wore. Its only colour was a little streak of blood trickling down her cheek from close by the right eye.

'Margaret!' he said again.

But she was breathing still. Her breast rose gently and evenly as though she slept: the pulse was regular, if not very strong. 'Only a knockout, thank God,' he thought. He struggled to his feet and, with the help of the seat cushions, arranged her more comfortably. Then he crossed to the window and looked out.

A nice sort of mess they were in. Something pretty final must have happened to the bunch of rocket tubes at the tail—and that meant the end of their motive power. There was no patching up to be done with rockets; either the system worked, or it was useless. It was lucky that there had been no pre-ignition—that would have meant nothing to show but a few scattered bits at the bottom of the New Sea. The *Sun Bird*'s hull had of necessity been airtight for stratosphere travel, and it still appeared to be at least watertight—anyhow, there was no sign of leakage yet. Almost certainly one of the mixing chambers for the gases had burst, either through overcharging or on account of a flaw in the casting, and the explosion had carried away the whole group of exhaust tubes, together with both sets of rudders.

They were floating high, with the entrance well clear of the water. He unfastened the door and pushed it open with the intention of climbing out on the wing to survey the damage. But nothing of either wing remained, save a few twisted rods projecting a foot or more from the plane's smooth side. Both must have been torn clean away by the force with which they had met the water. By means of considerable scrambling and with a series of efforts which made the pulses in his brain throb and hammer, he managed to use the fragmentary wing supports as a means of scaling the curved side. At last, perched on the roof, he was able fully to realise the predicament.

The stripped fuselage was rolling gently as it drifted aimlessly upon the rippled surface, no more, now, than a helpless metal hulk looking like a huge, elongated metal eggshell. The sun was already well down in the sky, and with its decline a slight breeze had risen from the north. A number of islands and palm clumps were within sight. Mark silently thanked God that they had fallen clear of them. Directly to the south a palm grove of several acres still survived. It was a bare mile and a half away and the wind was urging him slowly towards it.

He prayed that the direction would not change. He would feel far safer with his feet on dry land, for though the hull appeared sound enough, only a careful examination could make certain. For all he could now tell there might be a gush of water from a weakened spot at any moment.

By leaning cautiously over the side he was able to see through the window that the girl had not moved. His hesitation whether he should go down and attempt to revive her was settled by a sudden freshening of the breeze. It was not impossible that they might pass right by the island while he was busy, and though sandy hummocks broke the surface in plenty, no other islet in sight was of such reassuring size and height. To add to his uncertainty the wind veered a few points west and it became a nice point whether they would not miss the island by a good margin. He watched the narrowing space anxiously.

At a quarter of a mile it became certain that they would clear the most easterly spit by at least fifty yards. Mark decided to take a chance. It should be possible if he swam strongly to tow the wreck sufficiently to one side. He dropped overboard to find that the water came no higher than his armpits, for the islands were the remnants not of sudden hills, but of gradual undulations.

Towing the *Sun Bird* ashore proved a longer business than he had anticipated; a man three-quarters submerged has but little weight to give him purchase, and the task was made the harder by the fact that the Mediterranean water is salter and therefore more buoyant than that of the oceans. But the work grew progressively easier as the ground shelved until at last there came the welcome sound of the metal bottom grating on the sand. A few minutes later he had carried Margaret ashore and laid her in the shade of a tree.

A damp rag cooled her face and wiped away the trickle of blood. Her eyelids opened at last unsteadily, as though unwillingly, and the hazel eyes looked up into his. The arched brows straightened into hard lines and came together with deep creases between. Mark, with a sympathetic memory of his own blinding headache, offered a flask of brandy.

'Take some of this; it'll do you good.'

She drank without protest and closed her eyes once more. After a few minutes she looked at him again.

'I feel a bit better now. Let me sit up.'

'Certainly not. You lie here a bit longer. You've had a nasty bump.'

'What happened?' she asked.

Mark explained as far as he was able.

'If I hadn't been such a fool as to forget about the safety belts we should have been all right,' he added. 'As it is, I don't see why we haven't bust our skulls—I deserve to have done.'

'What are we going to do?'

'I don't know yet. We shall have to stay here for the night, anyhow. It'll be dark in half an hour. Tomorrow we'll see what can be managed. It depends mostly on the condition of the *Sun Bird*—poor old bus, that's a bit of a misnomer now: she'll certainly never fly again.' He looked regretfully at the silver hull gleaming in the last rays of the sun. 'There's a little tinned food and a small tank of water inside, so we needn't starve.' He looked back at her face a little anxiously. 'How are you feeling now?'

'Heaps better. Let me sit up.'

He was still uncertain how his news of the situation was being received.

'I'm damned sorry about all this——' he began.

She stopped him. 'My dear, you couldn't help it—and even if you could, I'm scarcely in a position to walk home.'

She was silent for some moments and he saw with surprise the beginning of a smile. He had been prepared for blame, reproaches, irritation, even calm acceptance of the situation—for anything, in fact, except a smile.

'Do you know,' she said, 'we've made a record?'

'What do you mean?'

'Well, nobody else has ever before achieved a shipwreck in the middle of the Sahara desert.'

Mark smiled too, and his spirits rose astonishingly.

'Come to that,' he said, 'I shouldn't think any girl was ever before kissed on a Saharan island.'

Mark suffered an uncomfortable dream. He had become, it appeared, a recumbent statue of himself, and was being dusted. A giant maidservant had removed her huge wig of red hair and was using it to whisk his face. She put one hand upon his stone chest for support, and leaned forward to reach the better. The hair irritated his nostrils abominably...

He woke suddenly. There was still a weight upon his chest, and something was still whisking back and forth across his nose. He sneezed abruptly and sat up, sending a dark form tumbling to the sand. There was a slight scutter before it collected its dignity and became a motionless black shadow in the moonlight. It gave a forth a faintly protesting mew. Mark looked at it unkindly.

'Blast you, cat,' he said, severely.

To a cat more used to kicks than words, this appeared a term of endearment. It approached and rubbed its head in a friendly way against his hand.

The New Sea was glittering with a hard beauty under the moon. A steely path of light stretched before him to the horizon over water which was scarcely rippled. A breeze, so light as hardly to be felt, caused the palm fronds above him to move with a papery rustling. He turned his head and saw with relief that the hulk of the *Sun Bird* still remained where he had left it.

A careful examination had proved it in better condition than he had hoped. The explosion had spent itself backward, ripping off the tail so smartly as to leave the main part of the fuselage intact. A few plates aft had been twisted open, revealing the sound-proofing material beneath, but in no part was there any sign of leakage. Reassured, he had insisted that Margaret should sleep on board. He contrived as comfortable a bed as possible for her, and, with the aid of severed control wires, he had improvised what he hoped were safe moorings. They seemed still to be holding.

He shivered slightly. The fire had dwindled to a few embers, and he leaned forward to build it up. Saharan nights can be chilly, and the fire served the double purpose of giving warmth and providing a signal.

There was no great likelihood of it being observed, but there remained always the possibility of a French observation plane cruising in this direction. They were used, he knew, to report progress and to effect salvage work upon occasion. The Government had frequently found it necessary to rescue diehards whom not even the threat of inundation had been able to persuade from their ancestral villages until the last moment. Among many of the Arabs understanding continued to fight with conviction. The French proposals were intelligible enough, but not a reality. Most of them felt that the desert always had been, and always would be; it was eternal. Not until the water crept to their very doors were they convinced. Only then did a howl go up demanding rescue either by Allah or the French Government. There had been a time when all the flying boats of both France and Italy had been pressed into refugee work, but, by now, the evacuation of most of the affected parts was complete.

With his head tilted back, Mark listened for the drone of an engine, but nothing broke the silence save the quiet stir of the sea and a faint swishing of the palm leaves. He wriggled nearer to the fire and pulled the coats which were doing rug duty more closely about him. Gazing at the revived flames he fell to considering the general cussedness of things. That the first time the *Sun Bird* had let him down, it should have chosen to do it in this no-man's-land....

Still, they had been lucky. If that explosion had occurred over dry land—or even at a good height above the water—it would have meant flowers for two. He thought of a number of well-pointed, nicely tempered phrases which he would joyfully plunge into the makers of 'Strato-planes' when he got home—not that it would do much good, but he would like them to hear just what he thought of them.

And then there was the radio.... Two reputedly unbreakable valves thoroughly broken, and the whole installation useless just when it was most needed....

The cat interrupted him by brushing past his face and making her way beneath his covering. She curled up comfortably and began to purr like a miniature massage machine.

'Oh, all right, if you insist,' he told her sleepily, 'but if you get overlayed, don't blame me.'

'Hi,' a voice was saying, 'what about breakfast?'

His eyes opened to the sight of Margaret bending over him. He struggled into a sitting position and blinked at a sun which had evidently been up for some time, then he transferred his gaze back to the girl. She had contrived to make herself scarcely less neat and fresh than she had been at the start.

'How do you do it?' he asked, feeling his own bristling chin.

She laughed. 'A bathe and a comb—but I do wish I'd brought a toothbrush.'

'How's the head?'

She shook it, spinning her hair out in the sunlight like a copper-gold halo.

'No sign of an ache—though there's still a bump like an egg. A sleep and a swim do wonders.'

The cat emerged. It took a firm stand with its forepaws, extended its hind legs so far that its loins almost touched the ground, and yawned immoderately. Seen by daylight, it was not a very attractive specimen of its kind. The surprising prominence of its eyes and the faded quality of its gingery coat were the two most noticeable characteristics.

'Where on earth did you find that?' Margaret asked.

'I didn't; it found me. Planted itself on me—literally.'

'Puss—puss,' Margaret encouraged.

The cat regarded her for a solemn moment. It decided to wash its face.

'There's ingratitude for you,' said Mark. 'There's nothing more egocentric than a cat.'

'Poor thing. They left it behind, and it might have been drowned. Let's adopt it.'

'If you like—but cats can wait. Let's see about some food. I'm feeling half-starved.'

The *Sun Bird*'s lockers supplied a number of brilliantly labelled tins.

'Grape fruit, tongue, some dates from the trees—oh, we won't do so badly. But I do wish we'd got some coffee—even the French idea of coffee wouldn't be too bad now. I hate tea for breakfast.'

Nevertheless, it was with a comfortable sense of repletion that they leaned back, enjoying cigarettes after the meal. Margaret watched the cat greedily consuming condensed milk.

'I think we'll call her Bast.'

'Why Bast?'

'You remember. The cat-headed goddess of the Egyptians—why, she may be a descendant of one of the actual cats they used to worship.'

'Highly probable. She has the manner—others might call it nerve. Henceforth, Bast she is.'

Margaret drew at her cigarette and changed the subject.

'What are we going to do? Just wait here?'

'I've been wondering about that,' Mark frowned. 'A patrol is bound to come along sooner or later—but the trouble is that we can't stay here for very long.'

'The sea?'

'Oh no. That's all right. The level rises so slowly that it won't flood this place for weeks, perhaps for months. No. I was thinking of the supply problem. We've got a little food, and there are the dates—though we'd soon get mighty sick of them—but the real trouble is drinking water. We've only got enough of that to last us two or three days. It really boils down to taking one risk or another. Either we stay here and chance their finding us before the water gives out, or else we try putting to sea in the poor old *Sun Bird.*'

'Putting to sea?'

'Don't look so surprised. She's perfectly watertight. I'm not proposing to be like the people who "went to sea in a sieve, they did"; not my idea of amusement, at all. We ought to be able to rig a sail of some kind. With that, and a means of steering, it would only be a matter of going right ahead till we find the shore. The sea's not really very big yet.'

Margaret looked uncertain.

'But suppose we land where there's nothing but desert?'

'I know. That's the real risk of the thing. The *Sun Bird* will be safe enough, but we may have to tramp over miles of sand at the end of the trip. What do you think?'

'Well, it's for you to decide, but if the *Sun Bird* is all right, it will be better to be doing something than just sitting and waiting, won't it? Besides, if a plane does happen to come along, it'll be more likely to see us out in the open than here.'

'You're right.' Mark scrambled to his feet and held out

a hand to her. 'Let's go down to the old bus and see what's to do about it. Come on, Bast, you too.'

It proved less difficult than he had anticipated to improvise a sail from a rug. True, it was so heavy that half a gale would be necessary to make it belly out, but it served its purpose by getting in the way of what wind there was. Progress with its help would be slow, but moderately sure. A plank and other bits of jetsam from the island strand could be adapted for use as a rudder.

Mark, looking back at his handiwork from the shore whither he had waded to collect a final supply of dates, laughed aloud. Many an odd ship had sailed the seas, but few craft odder than the transformed *Sun Bird*. It was a very good thing she was safer than she looked. If she had been an ordinary plane, now—but in that case neither Margaret nor himself would have been alive. . . .

'Come on, Bast, you're ship's cat from now on,' he said, picking her up and placing her upon his shoulder.

He gathered an armful of possessions and dates, and began to wade back.

The ex-control-wire mooring lines were hauled aboard; the ex-control-wire main-sheet shortened, and the good ship *Sun Bird* began slowly to move. Gradually she picked up, sliding reluctantly away from the shore.

'We're off,' said Margaret delightedly.

'Magnificent,' Mark agreed. 'We must be making almost a knot, and twice that in leeway. Just wait till we get clear of the island and can run before the wind. We'll show a turn of speed which would make snails blink.'

The two sat aft, perching none too steadily upon the polished, curving surface of the fuselage. Bast, unable to find any foothold save on the very crown, had been banished to the cabin for her own safety.

'It's lucky,' said Mark, 'that neither of us has any devoted relatives waiting for us at the Hôtel de l'Etoile—they'd be getting a bit restive by now, and at this rate we mayn't be home for weeks.'

Margaret looked up from her occupation of making a sunshade out of an old newspaper, and nodded.

'They certainly would. As it is, I suppose nobody's taking any interest except the manager who'll want his money, and a few romantic people who are now spreading a report that we've eloped or that you've abducted me.'

Some two hours later Mark sat alone at the helm. Margaret was below, contriving a meal. The lightest of breezes continued to move the *Sun Bird,* though at a distressing dawdle. Only the gentlest ripples troubled the surface of the water; their faint clopping against the bows and Margaret's voice raised in expostulation were the only sounds.

'Really, Bast,' she was saying, 'you're not quite a lady, are you. And on the very best cushion, too. I'm ashamed of you. If you dare to——'

A sudden noise occurred astern. A thud, a roar of falling water, followed by a great splashing. Mark looked behind him. He was just in time to see the spray from the impact of two waves falling back upon foaming froth. There were a few moments of uncertain agitation, and then the troubled water began to swirl. From its slow first turns it began to speed up until it dipped conically at the centre. The froth disappeared. The water circled yet faster, the sides of the deepening cone looking hard, like dark glass.

He put the tiller hard over in an effort to keep clear of the whirlpool, but its influence was extending. Already he could feel the drag of it, and the wind was too light to hold against it. The *Sun Bird* rocked, seemed for a second to hesitate and then gave up. Reluctantly she answered to the pull of the water and began to drift astern. A sudden terrifying roar broke out. Margaret's head appeared through the doorway.

'What——?' she began.

'Look out!' Mark shouted. 'I'm coming down.'

He slid swiftly down the side of the hull, swung himself through the opening and slammed the door behind him.

'What was it? It sounded like all the baths in creation running out at once.'

'Look there!' He pointed through the window, and together they peered out.

The *Sun Bird* was beginning to travel fast, close to the edge of the whirlpool. They could look right down into the hollow of spinning water.

'The bottom must have given way. Caves or something like that below.'

'Do you think——?'

'Can't say. There may be enough force to drag us down. Perhaps we'll just spin in the middle till it fills up.'

He drew her back from the window. She turned very wide eyes to stare into his.

'Oh, Mark, if——'

'Come on. We've got to strap ourselves into our seats. There'll be a hell of a mix-up in here if we do go down. Quick now.'

They both slid hastily into their seats and fumbled for the buckles of the broad webbing belts. The *Sun Bird* was circling the wall of water at a prodigious pace. She tore spirally down it to spin like a top at the centre. Mark hoped desperately. Would she . . . ? Would she . . . ?

She canted. The water rose dark over the windows. She swung abruptly, nose down. There was sudden, complete darkness inside. A sense of weightless dropping. Down and down. . . .

CHAPTER III

A WATCH would have told that the *Sun Bird* did not fall for many seconds—but seconds, infinitely drawn, mean nothing. She fell for an eternity. Uncannily like those dreams of Mark's childhood when he had slid faster and faster down a stair-rail which had neither beginning nor end. There was the same sense of plunging weightlessness; the same awful apprehension of the end.

But the end when it did come was, like so many ends, an anticlimax. There was a back pull as though brakes of unthinkable power had been applied to the full. The webbing safety belts were put to a strain which crushed the breath from their wearers' bodies. Mark could hear himself giving out involuntary, uncouth grunts. For a moment he feared that the belt might give and send him hurtling forward against the window, to smash or to be smashed. But the fabric held and the pressure swiftly eased. Presently he could draw a needed breath. Then abruptly the force reversed and they were thrust deep into their seats. 'Coming up again,' he told himself. The *Sun Bird,* carried to the depths by the fall, was rising bubble-like.

She broke the surface, spun like an ill-balanced top and was carried away broadside. He sat up and prepared to loosen the belt, but even as his fingers reached the buckle there came a thunder of water on the roof, loud despite the sound-proofing. The craft rolled like a floating barrel and sank again; rose again, and drifted back once more beneath the falls. She spun, twisted, rose and fell, like a wood chip beneath a weir. The brains of the two within swirled giddily.

'Nothing to do but hope,' Mark told himself. 'Bound to float free sooner or later.... My God, to think that they pay for things like this at fun-fairs.... Hope I'm not going to be ill.'

At last came a bump and a slight grating along one side. They could feel a slow, deliberate swinging. Mark waited for a moment, then:

'We're out of it,' he cried, unbuckling the strap. 'Where's that light switch?'

The small ceiling bulb revealed Margaret's slight form still sunk in the seat. She made a feeble attempt to smile at him.

'But I do feel sick,' she said plaintively.

'I'll bet you do. Just wait a minute while I find that flask.'

Bast emerged from the safe hiding of some corner, and stood looking at them from bemused, greenish-yellow eyes. She gave an unhappy mew and advanced towards Margaret. How she had contrived to remain undamaged was an unsolvable feline mystery.

The brandy which Mark at length produced had an immediate effect, not only of settling, but of heartening. Margaret loosed her safety belt and stood up. She staggered slightly.

'The ill treatment, not the drink,' she explained. 'Where are we? It's all dark outside.'

'Heaven only knows,' Mark managed, with an effect of lightness. 'A cave I should think, but it's a mighty big one to take a fall like that.' He pushed over a switch. 'Damn, the headlight's not working. Now where the devil did I stow those spare bulbs?'

He was convinced in his own mind that the end was not far off. The water from above would plunge down until the cave was filled. The *Sun Bird* would rise until she met the roof and could rise no more. The water would close round her, trapping them helplessly. The air in the storage cylinders would last them a few hours, and then . . .

'Ah, got 'em,' he said.

They were being rocked jerkily; swinging in a way which suggested that they were caught in a current, but the darkness outside was too intense to give even a hint of their surroundings. He crossed the cabin and opened the back of the headlight set above the front windows.

'Now,' he said, snapping it shut again with the new bulb in place, 'we'll be able to see just what we've fallen into.'

A brilliant beam slashed into the blackness. About them was swiftly flowing water, bearing them along. A few yards to the left was a rock-wall passing with surprising swiftness. Mark switched the light ahead, but there was little to be seen save the water swirling beside the rock until it disappeared into obscurity. To the right also the water stretched out beyond the lamp's range. Far above them the upsweeping curve of a rocky roof could be dimly seen.

Mark's spirits rose. At least, catastrophe seemed less imminent.

'Well, well, here we are. But where we are, and where we're going, the Lord alone knows,' he said.

He turned to look at the girl and his temporary spurt of lightness vanished. She caught sight of his expression and slipped her arm in his.

'Never mind, dear. It's not your fault. You couldn't know that the *Sun Bird* was going to misbehave like that, nor that this was going to happen. Besides we're both—well, we're in it together, aren't we?'

He looked down at her standing beside him. The white suit was sadly crumpled, a small, yellow bruise showed close to her right eye, the soft hair was a tangled, dark red disorder shot with gold lights, and the hazel eyes gazed steadily back at his own. He kissed her.

'You're lovely. And you're a brick,' he said.

A long time—or what seemed a long time—later, the right-hand wall of the cavern came dimly into view, converging rapidly to form a rocky tunnel ahead. Clearly this vast underground lake was narrowing to its exit. Mark focused the light forward, and viewed the prospect with no little misgiving. The speed of the water was perceptibly increased and the surface was broken by swirls and wavelets; it was impossible to tell how deep lay the rocks which must cause them. He wondered uneasily how long their luck would hold. One rocky spike could, at their present speed, rip the bottom from stem to stern. And to what were these rapids the prelude? Another fall would be likely to dash them to pieces. It had been mere luck that the earlier drop ended in a deep pool. Suppose a pile of rocks had lain beneath . . .?

The same thought was in Margaret's mind as she gazed frowningly forward; nevertheless, she managed to put some lightness into her tone as she spoke:

'I hope to goodness it's not another fall—I'm still feeling a bit sick from the last. I always thought that the people who go over Niagara in barrels were fools; now I know it.'

Mark drew her back from the windows.

'Better be on the safe side,' he said, pointing towards the seats.

The walls of the cavern closed in to leave a channel sixty or seventy feet wide. The *Sun Bird* was swept helplessly towards it, swinging and bobbing like a cork. Both held their breath as the course narrowed. It seemed impossible that they could safely clear the jutting spur at the left of the entrance. The stream gripped them, thrusting forward as if it could know no greater joy than to crush this metal eggshell upon sharp, savage rocks. Then, at the last moment, an outswirl of current deflected them. They were rushed past the spur with only a few inches to spare.

The searchlight had been left switched on, but it served only to heighten the effect of confusion. The beam flung erratically from side to side, confounding all sense of direction and giving every moment the impression that they were about to crash against one side or the other. Half a dozen times ominous scrapes on bottom or sides set their hearts pounding. One jolt after another convinced Mark that they were holed at last, but after each he was able to look round the cabin and see with relief that there was still no sign of leakage. It was a sharp cry from Margaret which managed, after twenty or more apprehensive minutes, to direct his attention farther ahead.

'Look!' she cried. 'Light!'

He stared through the forward windows. The motion made it difficult to be certain, but he seemed to catch a glimpse of a small patch of grey.

'Reflection,' he suggested.

'No, it's quite different. A colder, bluer kind of light than ours.'

He looked again, more carefully. The luminosity showed now in the shape of a high, almost Gothic, arch. 'As though,' he told himself, 'the end of this tunnel were silhouetted.' And its colour was, as Margaret had said, blue compared with the searchlight. Phosphorescence? But why should there be sudden phosphorescence? There was no trace of it in the water about them; a puzzle indeed, but soon to be solved, for their pace showed no sign of slackening.

He had to watch the opening grow larger and nearer for a longer time than he had expected. Distance in this darkness was deceptive, and his desire to be clear of the immediate dangers of the tunnel seemed to increase it. By the time they swished out upon a second lake, he felt that miles had been covered. They left their seats when the former jerky progress subsided into a smooth gliding, and stood close against the windows. The silence of astonishment was broken by Margaret.

'It's impossible! I don't believe it.'

Mark, too, felt that the scene was more like a dream than a reality.

They were gazing across a lake which filled one of the largest caverns he had ever seen. So large was it that he looked apprehensively above; it seemed incredible that such a span of rock could be sustained without the help of pillars. But the size of the place, the acres of subterranean water accounted for only a small part of their astonishment. The phenomenon at which they stared open-mouthed was a system of lighting, beyond any doubt artificial.

At regular intervals about the roof were set globes which had the appearance of being frosted glass. From each came a glow of soft intensity, a light which was blue-white, yet not dazzling.

Mark's earlier anxiety was supplanted by a fresh nervousness. The lights had been erected for some purpose. But what purpose? And by whom? Hitherto they had faced natural, and roughly calculable dangers. All had depended on the *Sun Bird*'s ability to survive; with her they had stood to live or perish. But with the discovery of the lights, a new element entered. They had been carried up against the unknown and, as always when all preconceived likelihoods are flouted, trepidation came crawling in. Men, he told himself, had put those lamps there—that could not be doubted. But what kind of men? What were men doing in these deep sunk caverns? Moreover, these glowing globes were unlike anything he had ever seen before—there was an entirely unfamiliar quality in the light they shed. As far as he could tell, they were a discovery not known above. What sort of reception might await intruders upon men who had for some reason hidden themselves deep and unsuspected in the earth? He glanced at Margaret, troubled. She was no longer gazing at the lamps; her attention had turned to the walls.

'Look, Mark,' she said, 'caves, there, above the waterline.'

He followed her pointing finger to see several openings, some near the water, others high in the wall, close to the roof. Moreover, he caught a detail which had escaped her. From the mouth of the largest a line of shadow ran slanting down into the water. A casual glance suggested a crack in the rock face; a longer look abolished the notion that it could be accidental.

'It's a ramp,' he said. 'A path leading up to that cave. . . .'

For a few seconds he hesitated. They were drifting slowly now, and their course would take them not far from the wall. A disinclination to leave the comparative safety of the *Sun Bird* fought with the idea of a possible way back to the surface. To stay on board meant that they would allow themselves to drift farther and deeper into this maze of caverns. Already an unknown number of hundreds of feet lay between them and the daylight, and there was no guarantee that the exit from this lake would not take them over another fall. On the other hand, who—or what—might they encounter in the caves?

It was a choice of unknowns, but with the balance slightly in favour of exploration. After all, they could moor the *Sun Bird*, and have her ready for retreat. If they were to go on, there might be no other chance of landing. He pulled off his coat, and sat down to loosen his shoes, giving instructions to Margaret as he tugged at the laces.

'I'm going to swim over to that ramp. I want you to get on top and throw me a line when you're near enough. The control wires we used for mooring should be long enough if you join them. Think you can manage?'

She nodded, and started to search for the wires. Mark opened the door and dived out without hesitation, within ten minutes the manoeuvre had been accomplished. Mark had caught the curling wire, and the *Sun Bird*'s metal belly was grating noisily as he pulled her bows on to the ramp. Margaret sprang down and stood beside him, watching him make fast.

'Isn't it quiet?' she said unhappily. 'I didn't think anywhere could be so horribly silent.'

Though she spoke in a low voice, the echoes managed to catch it and fling it eerily back and forth until it was no longer her voice, but a wandering, elemental sound. She shivered a little.

'I don't know which is worse; the silence, or the echoes.'

They listened for a moment to nothing. The silence sang in their ears with only an occasional clop-clopping of ripples to break it.

'Well,' said Mark cheerfully, 'as long as there's nothing but silence we needn't be afraid.'

The travesty which the jeering, booming echoes made of his statement seriously dismayed both of them. They glanced nervously at one another. Margaret took his arm.

'Do you really think we can get out that way?' she asked, looking up the ramp.

'Of course,' he managed with more conviction than he felt. 'The air's fresh here. There must be some way for it to circulate. If we can only——'

The rest of his sentence was drowned. There came the

rumbling of a mighty crash, thunderous in the closed space. The solid rock beneath their feet trembled. Mighty reverberations like great breakers of sound buffeted back and forth across the cavern lake. A hundred yards along the wall a poised mass of rock detached itself and fell deafeningly into the water. Margaret's grip tightened on his arm. He could see her mouth forming inaudible words.

'Look!' he shouted, pointing back at the tunnel through which they had come.

A sudden wave of frothing water came charging out to spend itself upon the broader surface of the lake.

'The roof must have dropped in. We were just in time: there's no going back that way.'

Margaret's alarm abated as the echoes became more feeble. She made an attempt to meet the latest calamity with lightness.

'Never mind, my dear. There never was. Only salmon can climb waterfalls.'

CHAPTER IV

'Now, have we got everything?' Mark said thoughtfully.

He looked in a calculating manner at the bundle beside him, and began to tick off the items on his fingers.

'Food, bottles of water, flashlights, string, matches, knife.... Lord, I nearly forgot...'

He slid from his seat and went to rummage in a locker. Margaret sat where she was, watching him extract a small pistol and drop it, along with a number of cartridge clips, into his pocket.

'Why?' she asked.

He shrugged his shoulders. 'I don't suppose we'll want it, but—well, it's better to have a pistol you don't want, than to want a pistol you've not got. We may run across—er—savage tribes or something when we get out.'

Margaret shook her head. The last sentence had been particularly unconvincing.

'Mark, you're trying to hide something from me. What

are you afraid of?'

'Nonsense. I'm not afraid of anything. What is there to be afraid of? I'm just being prepared, that's all—old boy scout motto.'

'Mark, don't be a fool. I don't in the least mind being protected, but I will not be treated as an idiot. What is it?'

He looked at her for a moment.

'Sorry,' he apologised. 'You're right, I was being a fool. I won't play at he-men any more. Quite frankly I don't know what to expect. It's all so queer. First the lights, obviously put here for a purpose—but for what purpose? And then this ramp which may have been partly natural, but has certainly been finished off by hand—and not in a day or two, either. Whoever did it has kept it a good secret from the people above. It's ten to one that they—er—well, that they probably want to keep it a secret.'

'They may kill us, you mean?'

'I can't possibly say—that's why I'm being prepared.'

'But, Mark, who can they be? Surely there would be some rumour or suspicion?'

'That's the queerest part of the whole thing. I never heard of mining operations or anything of the sort in these parts, did you?'

'Perhaps the French Government——?'

'I shouldn't think so—anyhow, we'll find out sooner or later. Let's get out now.'

They climbed from the *Sun Bird*, and he made to shut the door.

'No, wait a minute. We've forgotten——'

Margaret dashed back inside and reappeared with a wriggling bundle of fur.

'Poor Bast,' she said. 'We nearly left her to a dreadful fate. She'll have to come along with us.'

The cat mewed. Mark gave it a look of mild disapproval. It would probably be a damned nuisance; however, one could scarcely leave it to starve.

'Come on,' he said.

The ramp, an inclined ledge running along the face of the wall, was steep, but of no great length. A few minutes climbing was sufficient to bring them to its levelled off end in front of the cave mouth, and to show them a long tunnel illuminated at intervals by lamps similar to those over the water. Mark lingered only to cast down one regretful glance on the *Sun Bird* where she lay, glittering like a silver shuttle, at the water's edge. Then they turned their backs on the lake and entered the tunnel together.

For a time they walked in silence, each busy with thoughts. The floor had been smoothed and was dry, which made for easy progress. Both made efforts to convince themselves that it had an upward trend, but they were bound to admit that so slight a gradient would mean that many days walking lay between them and the surface. The monotonously echoed trudge of their feet began to get on Margaret's nerves. She glanced at the severely thoughtful expression on Mark's face.

'Well, what are you making of it?' she asked at length.

He started out of his reverie.

'Not much,' he admitted. 'I'm puzzled by that lake. Why on earth should anybody want to illuminate a lake? There weren't even any boats on it.'

'They may have been washed away.'

'But there would have been mooring rings or something to show that they'd been there.' He shook his head. 'And that ramp.... It didn't stop just below the surface; it went on and down, a long way. I wonder if——?'

'What?'

'Well, perhaps it has only just become a lake—it's more easy to understand that a huge, dry cavern should be lit like that. Suppose that the water from above has only recently broken through and flooded it?'

'Yes, that might be possible—I wonder——?'

They tramped on for a time without speaking. Mark's mind returned to the problem of the inhabitants. Where were they? And what manner of people could they be? Neither the corridor nor the lake had been lighted without purpose; yet there was no sign nor sound of a creature other than themselves. Their entire absence was becoming more uncanny.

The tunnel began to turn to the left. He consulted a pocket compass and learnt that they were travelling north. It could scarcely be called a useful discovery, but he was glad to know it; the tunnel must communicate with others, and the compass would at least serve to prevent them travelling in circles. It was not long before they came to a choice of ways; a tunnel, exactly similar to the one they were in, cut across at right angles.

'Toss up for it,' suggested Margaret.

Mark, after a careful inspection, came to the conclusion that hers was as good a way of choosing as any other.

'Heads, we go forward; tails, we turn.'

The coin spun and fell to the ground with a tinkle.

'Heads it is,' cried Margaret, looking down at the profile of Queen Elizabeth the Second. The way beyond the crossing differed from their earlier tunnel only in having a slight breeze which blew in their faces and grew perceptibly cooler as they advanced. It carried, moreover, the tang of some faintly familiar, though unplaceable, odour. They hastened their steps at the suspicion that the monotony of bare tunnels was soon to be broken. Keeping straight ahead, disregarding the smaller side tunnels which now became more frequent, they made for the source of the draught. The air became still damper and fresher. It carried a suggestion of growing plants. Nevertheless, the sight which met them when they turned the final corner took them by surprise.

As if by common consent they stopped on the threshold of a great cavern, staring in speechless amazement. At last:

'Mushrooms!' said Margaret, feebly.

Far, far up in the roof the familiar globes were shedding their soft rays, but this time they fell on to neither barren rock nor water; they served to show a nightmare picture. From a bed of dark, soft loam which covered the ground grew a huge crop of queer forms. Most massive, and most noticeable were mushrooms. Monstrous mushrooms which balanced umbrellaed heads larger than wagon wheels upon thick, white trunks, eight or nine feet high. Taller still reached the sleek cones of more slender fungi, yellow, red, or steely grey. Closer to the ground, among the pillar-like mushroom columns grew great globular plants, some brick red, some dappled brown and cream, some white, like familiar puff-balls, giantly inflated. Varie-hued tendrils, fat, like gorged serpents, lay here and there, contorted and looped by their efforts to find growing space. Shapes which, but for the virulence of their colouring, might have been marrows contrived to struggle for a compressed existence between the trunks and the swelling balls. There was chaos of line and form, but still worse of colour. The brushes of a distraught painter might have dabbed into the impossible scene the sudden splashes of purples, greens, reds, and yellows.

The sight of Mark's wide-mouthed astonishment made Margaret laugh.

'But it's incredible—fantastic,' he objected.

She nodded. 'Do you know what it reminds me of? Pictures in story books when I was a kid—only this technique's more modern. Enormous toadstools under which gnomes lived. There was one just like that in one book.' She indicated a particularly arrogant scarlet fungus, spotted with white. 'But I never thought I should see the real thing. Let's go nearer.'

They stepped from the firm rock border on to the loam, and examined the nearest mushroom curiously. Mark opened his knife and prodded it. It was quite soft. He sliced off a piece of the trunk and tasted it cautiously. The flavour was coarse, and the matter fibrous, nevertheless:

'It *is* mushroom, all right,' he admitted. 'If we can find anything to burn, we might make a fire and cook some.'

With Mark keeping a look out for a suitable specimen, they made their way farther along the edge of the weird forest.

'I suppose,' he said, 'that this is a kind of fungus farm, and that all these things are edible—but I'd rather not try them until we know for certain. I seem to have heard that you can eat lots of fungi if they're cooked the right way—the trouble is to know which is the right way.'

Margaret set the cat on the floor where it ran a little ahead of them, sniffing curiously at the thick stems.

'The more I see of this place,' she said, half to herself, 'the less I like it. First, unknown forms of light, and now this unthinkable fungus garden. Surely if men were mining down here they would have provisions sent down to them. They wouldn't choose to grow this stuff for food. It's quite certain that these things aren't natural; they've been forced, or developed, or something. How is it they're only grown here when they might have been commercialised up above?'

Mark grunted. He had grown tired for the moment of puzzling, and felt in a mood to accept what fortune offered. Here, for the taking, was food which would reinforce their meagre supply. Presently he found what he sought. A great mushroom, standing detached from the rest, on the fringe of the bed. It was easy to undercut it by hacking out large, white, pithy chunks.

'Stand clear!' he warned.

The giant toppled over with a thud. The head broke off and rolled free. He followed it and began to cut off manageable sections. While he was stooping, Margaret came up behind him. Her voice sounded odd:

'Mark, I'm going mad, or something.—There's one of the gnomes!'

'What?'

He spun round and stared at her. She had picked up Bast and was holding her in one arm. The other hand was pointing to a fungus which looked not unlike a dingy yellow beach umbrella. Motionless in its shadow, the queerest figure he had ever seen stood watching them.

Against the phantasmagoria of growths it was impossible to make an estimate of the watcher's size. Mark could only be certain that he was considerably shorter than himself. The unclothed body was covered with a skin which was grey-white, like dirty vellum. So lacking was it in pigmentation that it could not have known sunlight for many years, if at all. All four limbs were thin, though without emaciation; a not ill-formed, slender body was surmounted by an unusually round head. Two large, black eyes were gazing steadily and unblinkingly: they gave to the slightly negroid features an expression of deep and permanent melancholy. There was something in the racial type which stirred Mark's memory faintly; somewhere, either in a picture, or in real life, he was sure that he had seen faces stamped with just such an expression of unending sadness.

'Look, there's another,' Margaret nodded a little to the right.

He saw another figure hitherto unnoticed and all but invisible, so like was its bleached skin to the colour of the fungus trunks.

'And another—and another. Dozens of them,' she added.

Mark began to grow nervous beneath the unwavering stares. How long had these creatures been there? He wondered. Were there more of them even now prowling closer through the fungus thickets? He could feel the impact of all those dark, mournful eyes, following every detail of his movements. He looked questioningly at Margaret, She shook her tangled curls.

'My dear, I don't know. They don't seem very dangerous, do they? Perhaps they're only interested. . . .'

Mark thought. These queer folk must know the way to the surface—and they must be made to tell. They might intend no harm, but it would be better to make certain. He drew his pistol and assured himself that the magazine was full.

'We'd better get into the tunnel—it'll be less exposed,' he said, turning.

They had taken less than half a dozen steps when a rustle of movement came from among the fungi. An unseen signal put the white-grey men into simultaneous action. Mark, looking over his shoulder, was taken aback by their numbers; they showed in a score of unsuspected places, made visible now by movement.

'Run!' he cried.

A thudding of many bare feet sounded behind them, but they gained the tunnel mouth with a good lead. He stopped and faced round, putting Margaret behind him. The pistol was levelled threateningly; evidently it was known as a weapon, for they stopped short. He tried them in English.

'We want to get out. We want to go up,' he said, pointing to the roof.

The faces—nearly a hundred of them, he guessed—remained stolidly uncomprehending. He tried again. Pointing first to himself, and then again upwards.

'I—up,' he said hopefully, but the faces remained unencouraging.

'Oh, damn!' He glared angrily at them. Now that they were clear of the growths it became easier to judge their size; the tallest of them he put at about four feet six, though several stood no more than four feet.

'Try them in French,' he suggested to Margaret.

She stepped from behind him, with the cat still held in her arms. The effect was immediate and astonishing. Before she could open her mouth the little men grew suddenly excited. As if they had abruptly come to life, a buzz of chatter arose. Gesticulating arms pointed at her, expressions became animated. She turned back to Mark, disconcerted.

'What on earth——?' she began.

'Look out.' He dragged her roughly back.

The little men came forward at a run. He pulled his trigger viciously, firing blind into the press of their bodies. There could be no missing. A number dropped, and the charge checked. Several injured were screaming with pain. The reverberation of the shots was still echoing back and forth across the great cavern. The mingled uproar was awesome and unnerving after the silence. The still forms on the ground looked pathetically like those of children. Mark felt slightly sick, but he continued to brandish his pistol on the faces of the rest, waving them back. Margaret drew her breath with a sound which was half whimper. She forced her eyes from the fallen bodies and looked into his, horrified and part afraid.

'Oh, Mark, they're dead. You—you——'

He moved towards her and she shrunk back. The fear in her face was not of the little men.

'But, Margaret, I had to——'

'So suddenly,' she murmured. 'So horribly suddenly. A minute ago they were running, and now—— Oh, Mark, what have you done?'

Mark turned away. He hadn't intended to kill—only to stop. It wasn't really himself who had pulled that trigger so vengefully; something had taken hold of him ... oh, damnation....

The men had drawn off. Their faces were expressionless once more, and their eyes watched enigmatically. Perhaps he had been too hasty. Perhaps, as Margaret seemed to think, they had meant no harm. But he couldn't afford to let them come to grips on a mere 'perhaps'. Besides, there had been an air of determination about that charge....

He thrust a new clip into his pistol without ceasing to watch. They had started talking again in their queer, staccato tones. For the most part, their attention seemed to be directed at Margaret, though occasional apprehensive glances were thrown at his pistol. A deploying movement began. The crowd was stringing out in a semicircle about the tunnel mouth. He felt that they were contemplating a new rush. It would be impossible to hold off a charge spread over a hundred and eighty degrees.

From farther up the passage he might be able to hold them. He began to retreat backwards, never removing his eyes from their faces. But they did not advance at once. He wondered uncomfortably what was going on behind those sad, yet inexpressive faces.

He was a good thirty yards from the entrance before they moved. He saw a sudden stiffening run through them, then they were rushing headlong. His pistol spat viciously. The lead tore holes in their line. The noise of his shots in the confined space was a crashing, deafening roar which made his head sing. He could hear nothing else; certainly he had no suspicion of a hundred naked feet pattering behind him.

One choked cry from Margaret was all his warning, and it came too late. He went down even as he turned, in a rush of grey-skinned bodies. His pistol flew from his hand. His flailing legs and arms were seized and pinned down. A weight of squirming bodies was crushing the air from his lungs. Small fists clenched themselves in his hair and began to hammer the back of his head against the floor. Sickening, splitting thuds. There was a pain behind his eyes, hurting like the devil. His brain felt as though it were slopping about in its case like thin porridge....

PART II

CHAPTER I

CONSCIOUSNESS began to trickle back in a very filtered form. The first thing Mark was aware of was a familiar, blinding headache. He moved uneasily. There had been the explosion; the whole world turning somersaults; the *Sun Bird* diving at the sea.... No, that was farther off. Hadn't something else happened since then? He made a tremendous effort to open his eyes. Each lid seemed to be weighted with several pounds as well as being stiff from disuse. And when they lifted, he could not focus properly. There was a hazy vision of a grey surface which whirled and tilted. It steadied after a few seconds, and became clearer. Rock? That was familiar somehow....

Memory suddenly came back in full flood. The passages, the caves, the fantastic mushrooms, and the little men....

'Margaret?' he said feebly.

He turned his head, searching for her. He found himself lying in a cave the size of an ordinary dining-room. In the centre of the ceiling a blue-white lamp was glowing, smaller, but in other particulars like those in the corridors. Beside him, on the floor, stood a bowl of polished stone, full almost to the brim with water. He stretched out a hand to pull it closer, and then stopped in the middle of the action; the hand felt so weak, looked so thin and wasted that he could scarcely recognise it for his own. How long had he been here? he wondered as he leant over the bowl to drink.

The cool water did him good. He leaned his head back on the pillow and considered the surroundings more carefully.

The cave could hardly be called furnished, but someone had made attempts to render it habitable. Against the other walls were set low, couch-like mounds like that on which he himself lay. The coverings of both the small cushions and the larger which served for mattresses were woven from inch-wide strips of some strange material which was leather-like in colour, though not in texture. To give warmth and extra comfort somebody had wrapped a long, blue woollen scarf about him.

In several places the nakedness of the rock walls had been hidden by designs and pictures painted in three or four raw colours. But he noted that though the execution was rough, it was backed by knowledge; the crudity was in the workmanship, not in the observation. The study of a fungus forest was no less informed than the view of an Arab village, but there were figures here and there which puzzled him. Arabs he could recognize, white men and even the dwarf grey folk, but there were others, both men and women, which fitted into neither of these categories.

He raised a hand to his aching head and found that it was heavily bandaged. What had happened since that fight in the corridor? He had a misty notion of faces close to his own, voices which murmured encouragingly, but they had been strangers. Where was Margaret? He must find her....

The effort of sitting up set his head pounding again so that he had to clench his teeth. With difficulty he got to his feet and leaned for some swimming seconds against the wall. His legs felt so weakly useless that any movement might double them beneath him. The effort required to force them on was prodigious. Only his anxiety for Margaret drove him to make it.

The cave entrance had been chiselled to the shape of a doorway, though it held no door. It gave on to a corridor, dimly lit and stretching away to both sides. A faint murmur which might be of voices came from the right, and decided him to go that way. In all he made a journey of perhaps fifty yards, but it seemed one of the longest of his life. Four times in his slow course he was forced to rest against the wall, feeling too spent either to continue or return, wishing only to drop where he was. But each time he regathered, at last, just enough strength to drag his unsteady feet forward.

Finally the passage gave on to a cavern. He stood looking at numbers of men and women who crossed its floor on the way from one tunnel mouth to another. He tried to call out to them, but his voice sounded childishly weak. And something queer was happening to the people.... They seemed to be swimming about.... The whole cave was reeling drunkenly. His knees suddenly sagged. The floor of the cavern rose obliquely from the left, and hit him.

Arms lifted him into a sitting position; a smooth something was thrust against his lips.

'Here, drink this,' said a voice.

He obeyed feebly. A gulp of some coarse spirit burned its way down. His eyes opened to the hazy sight of two bearded faces hanging over his own. The mouth in one opened:

'What are you doing out here?'

'Margaret,' he managed to say. 'Where is she?'

The two bearded faces looked at one another. The first spoke again.

'That's all right, buddy. Don't you worry. All you got to do is rest. How about getting back now?'

They assisted him to his feet.

'Think you can walk?'

He nodded dumbly, but at the first faltering step his knees doubled up again. The taller of the two men picked him up easily, and strode back along the passage. Very thankfully Mark felt himself laid down on the couch he had so lately left. After an indefinite period which might have been a few minutes or a few hours, someone roused him. The man who had carried him was holding out two bowls, one containing water, and the other, a kind of mash.

'What——?' he began. But the other shook his head.

'No, just you get outside this first. You can talk after.'

He took a drink of water and started on the mash. It had a slightly earthy flavour, curious, though not unpleasant. While he fed he took stock once more of his surroundings. He was back in the decorated cave, all right, but this time he had three companions. The man who had spoken was a tall, broad figure, clad in the rags of a French uniform. His hands, and such parts of his face as were visible behind a matted beard, were lined with ingrained grime. Hair which might be fair when clean had been clumsily restrained, possibly with the aid of a knife. Above it, far back on the head was perched a battered képi.

Wonderingly, Mark transferred his gaze to the next. A slighter man, this, with hair thinning, though such as did grow had been lopped in the same crude fashion. His beard, like the others, was matted, and his hands equally grimy, but his clothing was different. The tatters of his suit would never be recognised by its London maker, but they were tatters of good quality. The third man was an Arab, wearing a burnous which had the appearance of having served its owner throughout an arduous campaign. It reminded Mark vaguely of certain battle-torn flags he had seen hung in churches.

He finished the mash, in which he detected traces of the same coarse spirit which had been given him before, and pushed the bowl away. He felt greatly improved. In a pocket he found a packet of cigarettes which he handed round. The three men looked at him as if he had performed a miracle. They lit up with a care which was almost reverent.

'Now perhaps you'll tell me where she is?' he asked.

'Was she with you?' inquired the big man.

'Of course she was. Do you mean you've not seen her?' He looked questioningly at them in turn. They shook their heads.

'But she was with me when I was knocked out. I've got to find her.'

He began to struggle to his feet. The tall man caught his arm and pushed him back.

'No. You keep sitting awhile. There's a whole lot you got to learn yet. And one of 'em is that it ain't no sort of good being in a hurry in these parts.'

'But——'

'I tell you, you can't do a thing. Anyway, you're still sick, and got to lay up for a bit. Take it from me, if your girl's safe now, she'll stay safe.'

'You mean that?'

'Sure I mean it.'

Mark believed him. The man spoke firmly, as though he had no doubt. Moreover, in his present state of weakness, he could be of assistance to no one. He dropped back on his cushions and contemplated the three.

'Well, for God's sake tell me something about this

place. I've been living in a kind of nightmare. I don't know how long I've been here, or even where I really am.'

'Well, you're the latest arrival, I can tell you that, though you've been sick a goodish time. You're a tailor's dummy to the rest of us in this dump. How d'you get here? Tell us your yarn first.'

Mark told his story in considerable detail. The first part seemed to hold more interest for his listeners than did the account of the fungus forest, and the tall man quelled the very evident desires of the European to make frequent interruptions. He was silent for a time after Mark's account of the fight.

'So that's what it's all about,' he said thoughtfully. 'No wonder the poor devils are getting all het up. It'll mean the end of them.'

'And of us too,' said the other.

The Arab merely nodded.

'But what are you doing here?' Mark asked impatiently. 'You're American, aren't you? Why the French uniform?'

'Say, we've forgotten the introductions. I'm John Smith, leastways that's my name in the Legion. This is Charles Gordon, of London, England, and this, Mahmud el Jizzah, of some God-forsaken hole in the desert. Gordon is an arch—, arch—, anyway, he digs for things which aren't no manner of good to anybody. And Mahmud, well I don't know what he does, but he was educated in some swell place in England, Oxford College.'

'Balliol,' murmured the Arab, deprecatingly.

'But what are you all doing here?'

'Just living here.'

'But why?'

'Because we darn well can't do nothing else. D'you think we're here for fun?'

Mark looked at their beards, and the rags which flapped about them.

'How long have you been here?'

'What's the date?'

Mark considered. Probably several days had elapsed during his unconsciousness, but he could remember the date of the *Sun Bird*'s crash.

'It was the sixteenth of September when we fell in.'
'The year, man.'
He stared. 'Why, 1964, of course.'
'That makes six years for me.'
'Seven for me,' said Gordon.
'Five,' admitted the Arab.
Mark's eyes opened wide. He looked from face to face for a sign that this was a leg pull.
'Seven years!' He stared at Gordon. 'You can't mean it. Seven years—here, in these caves?'
The other nodded and smiled a little grimly. 'Oh yes, I mean it, all right.'
'But—but I don't understand. There must be ways out.'
'There are ways out—must be any amount of them. The trouble is that we can't get at them.'
'Why not? You found your ways in.'
'So did you, but it doesn't help, does it?'
'But you didn't all come in down waterfalls.'
'No. The real trouble is these little grey guys. They've got us penned up like we was cattle. And haven't they just got the drop on us. Say, it'd be easier to crash out of hell than out of this joint.'
'But you don't mean you're here for good?'
'You've said it, buddy. You too.'
'But——'
Mark was aware again of the feeling that this was all part of a nightmare, growing worse at every turn. Imprisoned in these caves for the rest of one's life! It was fantastic, it couldn't be true. He turned to Gordon who was staring at the picture of the Arab village. There was something in his expression more disturbing than an hour of the American's conversation.
'It is quite true,' the Arab's voice assured him calmly.
'It can't be true. There must be a way out.'
'If anyone had ever got out, this place would no longer be secure. That it *is* secret means that no one ever has got out.'
Gordon interrupted. 'No, that's not so. I believe in my theory that——'
'Oh, damn your theories,' Smith cut in. 'Even if they're right, what the hell's the good of them to us? Cut 'em out.'

He turned back to Mark. 'The sooner you get a hold on the idea that you and me and all of us are in the cooler for keeps, the easier it's gonna be for you.'

Mark's convalescence was a long business. When it irked him, and he grumbled at the waste of time, Gordon did his best to be reassuring.

'For one thing, the phrase "waste of time" has no meaning in here,' he said. 'And, for another, you're damned lucky to be convalescent at all. Candidly, you were in such a mess when you came in that we never thought you'd make it. Then you didn't help things by getting out of here the minute you came round—it gave you a nasty relapse. Just lie there quietly, and don't fret about things. It won't do you any good to get what Smith calls "all het up".'

Mark did his best to obey, and during the time which followed, he came to know the three men well. His first hazy impressions had to be revised. Smith, for instance, was not altogether the pessimist he had appeared. So far from losing all hopes of escaping from the caves, as he had suggested, he was full of hopes. His insistence on its impossibility was seldom a genuine belief; far more often it was a defence, a kind of counter-suggestion set up to check his hopes from rising too high. Once, in a moment of unusual confidence, he admitted:

'If I didn't think we were going to get clear of this place sometime, I guess I'd have bumped myself off before now; but if I let myself get too worked up, I'll probably have to bump myself off one day through sheer disappointment. Most of the time I expect the worst; it's so good when it doesn't happen.'

A simple theory, Smith's, of not tempting the gods. It had points in common with the practice of carrying an umbrella to persuade the sun to shine, or travelling with two spare wheels in order to avoid a puncture. Beneath his attempts to bluff fate, he was more hopeful than the others.

Gordon had reached a mental stage verging upon acceptance of the inevitable. Only a firm belief in some of his theories—of which, Mark was to discover, he had many—had prevented him from long ago relinquishing all idea of return. Even so, he was not likely to sink into the despair which Smith feared. He had a power of dissociating himself from his surroundings and losing himself in the purely conjectural, without which he would indeed have been forlorn. He was not without moods of deep dejection, but even a chance word would often break their spell. A light of sudden excitement would flicker in his eyes, the thin face would come to life as though a mask had been cast off, and in a few moments he would be holding forth violently; passionately advocating theories which were sometimes sound common sense, and at others the extreme of fantasy. For the most part his words seemed to flow around Smith without causing a ripple of appreciation; though occasionally the big man would grasp a practical suggestion out of the flood of words, and haul it ashore with satisfaction.

The Arab listened to the talk with little more comment than a grunt here and there. Mark was uncertain whether his silence covered fatalistic acceptance, or profound thought. Whichever it was, he seemed of all the party, the least affected by the situation. When he did talk it was usually to give reminiscences or to tell some Arab fable of which the point was completely incomprehensible to the European mind. His chief link with the others seemed to be a mutual admiration between Smith and himself. The big frame and the slow strength of the American found its complement in the wiry agility of the Arab.

Mark, growing stronger, began to develop a more active interest in his surroundings, and a desire to know how he came to be in his present company. His own method of entry was, beyond doubt, unique. He demanded to know how Smith had found his way in.

Smith pulled his car thoughtfully, and looked at the others with some doubt. Mark realised that the three must know one another's stories by heart.

'I don't mind. Carry on,' said Gordon, and the Arab nodded amiably.

'Well, it ain't much of a yarn, but here it is. We—a company of us, that is—had been moved up to do some police work in the mountains north of Ghardaia—and let me tell you that if you don't know where Ghardaia is, you ain't missed much.

'Now, the Frenchies have an idea that a guy who's still

alive after a couple of months in the Legion is so tough that he can't be killed anyway. And they behave according. They dress you up in the heaviest clothes they can find, give you a camel-sized pack and send you hiking for thousands of kilometres where the sun's shining twice as hot as it does any place else. I can't say how many blasted, blistering miles we put away that day, but I do know they marched us till we was pretty near dead. Some of the poor devils were all but asleep on their feet, and I was as near all in as makes no difference.

'I guess they didn't mean us to fight. The big idea was to make a nice bright show of uniforms, and whatever local sheik it was that had gotten a bit above himself would just naturally curl up and reflect on the glory of *la France*. Yes, that was the idea, right enough. The trouble was the Arabs didn't see it that way—maybe the uniforms didn't look smart enough, or something. Anyway, they waited till we were about played out, and then took a hand. We were in the open, and they were on the cliffs above us, skipping about just like antelopes—'cept that they had guns—and taking playful pot shots—most of 'em bulls. It wasn't so funny, and we got orders to do the only possible thing—leg it to the cliff foot and take cover.

'There were a lot of caves there, all sizes, and not wanting to stay outside and have rocks dropped on our nuts, we made for 'em. And there we stayed put. They'd got us all nicely bottled up, and how! All you'd got to do for a fatal dose of lead poisoning was to take one look outside. Some guys who'd been told that Arabs can't shoot tried it—once.

'Maybe it sounds worse than it looked. Anyway, we weren't worrying a lot—I reckon we all just wanted to sleep. It wouldn't be long before somebody at headquarters missed us and started raising hell to know what we were at. We'd nothing to do bar sit tight and wait.

'But the local sheik didn't see the fun of that. He'd started something, and he was going through with it. It'd probably be easier for him to explain away the disappearance of a whole company than to account for a few dead bodies. He was wholesale-minded, that fellow. We'd been there about an hour when there was hell's own crash, away on the right. A couple of our men looked out to see what had happened—maybe they did, but it wasn't much help to us, seeing that they got bullets through their heads for their trouble. The rest of us were content to sit tight and guess what particular form of hell-raising was going on outside. A half-hour later we knew for certain. There was a Gawdalmighty explosion right above us. Half the cliff face must have split off and come down with a run. Leastways, it was enough to bury the mouth of our cave, and put paid to four poor devils who were standing near. The wily sheik had hit on a swell idea for covering up his tracks, and it looked like we were buried alive.... I reckon the guys in the other caves were; I ain't seen none of 'em in these parts.

'Well, that left three of us standing. Olsen, Dubois, and me. And we had the choice of sitting down to die right there, or looking round the cave to see whether there wasn't some other way out. We hadn't a hope of shifting the tons of stuff in the entrance. After a bit we found a kind of a crack at the back. There was a draught through it, which meant it went some place. We shoved in and started hiking again, with a few bits of candle between us.

'I don't know how long it was before Olsen and me found ourselves looking down a split into one of those lighted tunnels—some days, most likely. And it's no good my telling you the way those lights struck us; you must've felt the same way yourself when you first saw 'em. If it hadn't been that Olsen saw 'em, same as me, I'd 've thought I was nuts.

'We'd lost Dubois. He'd fallen into a crevice some place back along, and broken his neck—poor devil. Olsen wasn't in too good shape, either; he'd broken an arm, and pretty near knocked himself silly on a stalactite. But we'd made it—just.

'A bunch of them white pygmies found us wandering around. They didn't seem much surprised to see us. They brought up some food, and let us sleep a bit, then they marched us off here.'

He stopped. Apparently he considered his tale was finished. From Mark's point of view, it was scarcely begun.

'But what is this place?' he prompted. 'You forget I've seen practically nothing of it except this particular cave.'

'This? Oh well, you could call it a kind of jail. It's a corner of their system of caves, and there's only one way in to it. You were "out" when they lugged you along, or you'd have seen the way it is. They brought you down a tunnel much the same as the rest, only it stops short on a ledge. And that ledge is about a hundred feet up the side of one of the biggest of our caves. There's no ramp, nor steps, nor nothing leading from it. They just put a rope round you and let you down in here, and that's that. You can't climb up a hundred feet of smooth rock—not even if you're a human fly.'

'But do you mean to say that nobody's tried to get up?'

'Tried? By gosh, they have. But there's always some of the little grey guys watching for 'em. There's marks near the bottom where somebody had a try at cutting handholes—they say he was stopped by a rock being dropped on his head. I once saw a fellow try to make a break for it. Frenchie, he was, and about half crazed, or he'd never have tried it. They'd just let down a new specimen into this corral when this guy thinks he sees a chance. He rushes out of the crowd of us watching, grabs the rope and starts climbing like a monkey. They let him get three-quarters of the way up before they cut the rope.'

Mark remained almost as puzzled as before. Smith had been so long below ground that he failed to understand the bewilderment of a newcomer. Familiarity had wiped away his earlier amazement at this system of caves. Its existence had become an accepted, unsurprising fact, and the life within it a misfortune rather than an astonishment.

'But who are these little white men? What are they doing here? Why don't they come out?'

The American shook his head.

'That's out of my line. Gordon has a theory about it. Get him to tell you some time. What's interesting me right now is the dope you gave us. It makes things clearer.'

'I gave you?'

'Sure. The low down on this New Sea stuff. There's been something worrying them, we've seen that, but we couldn't figure out just what it was. Now we've got it.'

'Does it help?'

'Help? Oh, it helps all right. It means when we get drowned down here we won't have to worry any more about getting out.'

Another time Mark put his questions to Gordon with greater success. The archaeologist, though he had been imprisoned longer than Smith, had contrived to keep his mind more supple. Not only had he retained an active interest, save for brief periods of depression, in the whys and wherefores of this subterranean race and its origin, but he possessed some capacity for seeing another's point of view—a quality which could never have been characteristic of the American. Requests for information which Smith met with the assurance that there was 'no hurry' and that Mark would have 'a hell of a long time to find it out in', were treated by Gordon with some appreciation of the newcomer's bewilderment. He enlarged upon Smith's remark that their quarters were a 'kind of jail'.

'We're in prison for safety,' he explained. 'Our safety, and theirs. There are two good ways of making a man keep a secret; one is to stop his mouth, and the other, to stop his heart. Why they choose the former, I can't tell you, they don't seem squeamish about things like that. Anyhow, this way's just as effective, and it costs them nothing. We've got our own fungus caves, and we grow our own food in them. In fact the only real difference between their position and ours is that they can go out, but don't want to, while we want to, but can't.'

'How many are there in here?'

'It was somewhere about fifteen hundred last time we counted.'

Mark, who had thought from the way the others talked that fifty or a hundred might be a likely estimate, stared. Fifteen hundred——?

'You *do* mean prisoners?'

'Yes, prisoners. Counting all kinds. You'll see them as soon as you're strong enough to get about a bit.' Gordon spoke for once in a way irritatingly reminiscent of Smith.

'And none have ever escaped?'

'That's what they tell us, but I think they're wrong there. It was probably a devil of a long time ago, but I think it's been done—more than once.'

'Why?'

'Well,' Gordon frowned slightly, 'mind you, this is only a theory. I don't say that the facts might not be explained another way, but I hold that it is a possible explanation. You remember that you saw a fungus forest?'

'Yes?'

'What did it remind you of?'

'I don't quite——'

'Didn't it seem somehow familiar—as if you might have seen it before somewhere?'

Mark fancied he saw what the man was driving at. He remembered how Margaret had remarked on their likeness to toadstools in a story-book picture. Gordon beamed when he heard it.

'And what did she think of the white pygmies?'

'That they looked like gnomes—only they had no beards.'

The other spread his hands in showman style.

'Well, there you are. You *did* in some degree recognise the situation—it was not entirely unfamiliar to you although you thought it was. And what does that mean?'

Mark, not having the least idea of what it might or might not mean, remained silent. Gordon continued:

'It means that some suspicion, some faint rumour of such a place has leaked out into the world. All folk-beliefs have a rational beginning somewhere if you can find it. Men didn't invent the tales of gnomes and trolls, nor the idea of giant toadstools. Someone had the tale from a man who had actually *seen* them—several men, perhaps, for the legends are widespread. In the course of time the stories became garbled, and at the hands of painters our pygmies underwent a transformation, but they were still dwarfs, and in most places were reported as being unfriendly to ordinary men.

'I tell you, our pygmies are the originals. Centuries ago somebody who had been in here did get back to the world and tell them about it.'

Mark looked extremely doubtful.

'But nobody would have believed it—they'd have laughed them down. Just think what they'd say of us if we got out and told them about this without any proof.'

'You're getting your crowd psychology wrong. More

primitive people were wiser in some ways than we are. They did not jeer at everything outside the immediate realities. The mass attitude right up to the Middle Ages was to believe until an assertion was disproved (and in some matters that attitude still persists), but the typically modern attitude is to disbelieve until proof is forthcoming. In the old days people believed in the sea-serpent, nowadays they wouldn't believe in a kangaroo without photographs. They can still be hoaxed, of course, but the method has to be different. Besides, think of the peasants of old Europe; why should they be more surprised by hearing of small men who lived underground than by travellers' tales of men with black skins who went naked? One is as credible as the other. The difference is that in the course of time one tale became substantiated, while the other for lack of evidence to support it decayed into what is called folk-lore. Just suppose the blacks had killed every white man they saw, wouldn't their existence have become a myth, just as this people's has? Of course it would.'

Mark, confronted for the first time with one of Gordon's theories, felt that while it was extremely plausible, it was also extremely unconvincing. He avoided expressing his opinion by temporising.

'Then you think no one has escaped for a long time—perhaps several centuries?'

Gordon shrugged his shoulders. 'Impossible to say. They may have done. But, if so, there ought at least to have been rumours—tales among the Arabs. There may be, of course, but it is strange that we've never heard any. The most I can say is that I am convinced that there have been escapes in the past.'

'And if then, why not now?'

'Any of a dozen reasons. They may have found the loophole and blocked it. These may not be the same prison caves. I must confess that the thing which puzzles me most is why they don't kill us as they find us, and have done with it—but then, different races always have their own funny ideas on the subject of killing....'

CHAPTER II

IT was with Gordon as guide that Mark made his first trip into the larger caves. The former had seen that further forced inaction would do Mark little good. Gradually returning strength had found its outlet in fretting and worrying. He asked continually and fruitlessly for news of Margaret, and the fact that all three of the men assured him that they had made every possible inquiry without success, did not tend to ease his mind. Even Gordon could make no suggestion.

'I never heard of such a thing before,' he admitted. 'Quite invariably every member of a captured party has been brought here and left to make the best of it, but I assure you she is not in any of our caves—it couldn't be kept quiet. Every newcomer is a centre of interest.'

'That's so,' Smith agreed. 'If it hadn't been that you got treated so rough, we couldn't have kept them off questioning you. Nobody's got her hid away; that's certain.'

'You don't think they—killed her?'

'No, why should they?' Smith spoke heartily; the other two said nothing.

Mark was without any means of telling how long he had lain ill. Night and day were not recognisable divisions in the caves; and with them went all other measures of time. One fed when hungry, slept when tired. Time flowed smoothly by in one long monotony. Days, months, years even, passed unrecorded save when a new arrival like himself reminded the prisoners that there was still an outside world where dates were kept. Each one was eagerly questioned for the current year and month, estimates were made of the length of time since capture, and then forgotten until another news bearer should arrive. The blue-white globes were never darkened, and their continual light had come to be accepted by the majority without wonder or interest.

Gordon admitted that his curiosity had led him to break one which he filched from a little used corner soon after his arrival. It had required a great deal of pounding with a heavy stone:

'Just curiosity, but it didn't get me anywhere. There was a splash of some kind of liquid on the floor. It shone for a while and then evaporated. The outside was pretty much like glass, only far tougher.'

'But doesn't that show that they had a pretty high development at one time, even if they haven't got it now?' Mark suggested.

Gordon was inclined to think that it didn't mean a great deal. There was no doubt that the pygmies were on the downward grade now, but it didn't seem likely that their level of civilisation could ever have been high. They had shown immense determination in constructing their labyrinths, enlarging and altering, until it was difficult to tell how much was natural and how much artificial, but in the matter of the light:

'It may have been just a fluke—one of those discoveries which are made and then forgotten. Think of Hero's steam engine at Alexandria, everybody forgot that for two thousand years. And those perpetual motion wheels which obviously weren't perpetual motion, but certainly worked somehow—they managed to get forgotten, unexplained. It happens again and again. Anyhow, there's nothing miraculous about these lamps. They wear out in time. You'll see some perceptibly duller than others.'

'All the same, I'll bet they'd astonish our physicists,' said Mark.

He became aware that he thought mostly as if he were a visitor to this place, a tourist; it was still impossible to realise that he might never come out, and he dreaded the moment when that realisation should be driven home. Perhaps it never would. Smith, after six years of it, was at bottom still unconvinced that he would die in this warren.

It was in such moods that he would revert to useless, frightening speculation upon Margaret's fate until increasingly frequent periods of restless irritation decided Gordon that even though incompletely recovered, he must be taken out of himself. He led him, still bandaged of head, and weakly in body to the big cave which he had glimpsed before. He stared silently at the scene for some minutes.

In addition to the figures which crossed between the various tunnel mouths, there were some sixty or seventy persons in the place. They stood or sat for the most part in groups, conversing in a desultory, uninterested fashion. An air of listlessness seemed to hang over them all; a lethargy which suggested that nothing need be done until tomorrow—and here there was no tomorrow. Their eyes, utterly lacking in spirit, looked as if they scarcely saw. The discouragement in their bearing was their most common possession; beyond that, variation was infinite.

Arabs predominated slightly, but whites of all types were numerous. A number of Negroes was scattered here and there, and even a few Indians could be seen, but there were some whom he could fit into no known category.

'What on earth is he?' he asked Gordon, pointing to one of these.

The man he indicated was as tall as himself and wore a minimum of clothing upon his grey body.

'Oh, he's a "native".'

'A native? I thought they were all small—you called them pygmies.'

'I don't mean a pygmy. By a "native" we mean one who was born here, in the prison caves.'

'Good God, you don't mean to say——?'

'Of course I do. There's quite a fair sprinkling of women down here, as you see. And you can't stop men and women being men and women, even in caves.'

'But to bear a child here——'

'I know. It seems pretty rough on the kid to us, but they don't think of it that way. The kid's an unavoidable accident from their point of view. Besides, the "natives" quite rightly say, why should they be condemned to perpetual chastity?—aren't things bad enough for them anyhow?'

'You mean that a "native" may have "native" parents?'

'That's it. By the look of that one, I should say he has.'

Mark watched the man out of sight. He felt shocked. A man who had never seen sun or stars; never heard waves breaking or trees rustling; never seen a bird, never—oh, it was endless. And Gordon made the statement so calmly. Had he forgotten what the outside world was like? Had he stifled his memories all these seven years? It seemed more likely that a man would dwell upon them until he remembered the surface as a paradise. What was it Smith had said the other day—no, there were no days here—what was it he had said a little while ago? He had been more abstracted than Mark had previously known him. There had been a dreamy longing in his manner of speaking.

'Bored! My God, to think that I could ever have been bored up there. Why, right now I could look at one flower for a week, and still find it marvellous. I used to reckon old man Wordsworth was kind of soft; I guess I was out there. Daffodils! Just think of 'em; a bank of 'em, blowin' in the wind!'

To him the world had become a flower garden, and the sky was for ever breaking into sunset. Sentimental? Of course it was sentimental, but it seemed a more natural state than the insensitiveness Gordon displayed. He was talking now about the natives coldly, dispassionately, as though they were museum exhibits:

'It's one of the drawbacks man suffers for his adaptability. Many another kind of creature shut up like this would die, pine away from sheer discouragement, but not man. Given time, these "natives" would evolve into a race perfectly adapted for this environment.' He paused, and glanced at Mark. 'You think that that man we saw a moment ago suffers a sense of loss. You imagine him deprived of his birthright—well, perhaps he is, perhaps we all are, but does he know it? Do we know it? What are these rights of man? That man never knew the open air, and he doesn't want to. He can't understand anything but life in caves. How should he?'

'But he must know. He must have heard from you and the rest of them here.'

'Of course he has, but it doesn't touch him. Doubtless your parents told you plenty about heaven—how beautiful it was, and all the rest of it, but how does that strike you now? Pretty thin, pretty much of a fairy-tale? Well, that's the way he feels when he hears of the world outside—a pleasant, rather childish fancy with little or no real significance. He hears about sky and fields and clouds and mountains just like you heard about harps and angels and streets paved with gold—and he takes about the same amount of notice.'

Mark frowned. He saw what Gordon was intending: the philosophy of 'what you've never had, you never miss'. But that, to his mind, was a shallow view. Carried to a logical extreme it would mean that man was a static creation, whereas he was the most dynamic. Indubitably man could, and did, miss what he had never had, the whole history of invention was a record of his attempts to overcome recognised deficiencies. He had never flown, but he missed the power of flight; the aeroplane was evolved. He lacked the ability to live for days on end in the water; the ship was built. His own unaided voice could only carry a short distance; intricate systems of communication were brought into being. It was nonsense. One could be aware of a restraint from within it. But the arguments bounced off Gordon. Mark's instances, he claimed, were superficial.

'For the most part they are imitative and cumbrous. Look at the complications needed to broadcast a message, and compare it with the simplicity by which a flock of migratory birds knows of its meeting-place, and the time of its flight.'

'But the very fact that we can broadcast, shows that we have recognised our limitation.'

'Does it? I doubt it. I should say that we recognised it as a limitation of the system we have evolved, not of ourselves. We put up an inferior substitute called telegraph and radio, and forget our limitations—but they are still there. How many men, do you suppose, realise the limitations of using words to convey our meanings? They may find that there are inconvenient misunderstandings, and blame language, but how many admit that the words are just a substitute for the thing they really lack—mental communication? Precious few. My point is that they do not realise the lack of direct mental communication, because they've never had it. They look on spoken or written language as a natural method of expression, whereas it is really a mechanical process more complicated than radio.'

'Yes, but you can't get over the fact that they have evolved a process to fulfil a need. And if that isn't a sign of recognising limitation, what is?'

'In some degree, but it is not *fully* recognised. There is a kind of mental myopia. Look at what happened. First there was the very arduous invention of the spoken language. Then it was seen that this only had a limited use—it could travel no great distance in either space or time—so there grew up a written language. This failed to reach enough persons in a short time; printing became necessary. In an effort to decrease the time-lag still further, electric communications followed. And all this process had to be gone through (and will be further elaborated) because the limitation was not clearly perceived in the beginning. The thing we really lacked was direct mental communication.'

'But that's impossible.' Mark was growing irritated.

Gordon's serious face relaxed into a sudden grin.

'Splendid. In effect, that's the power we've never had, and because we've never had it, you think we never will—practically "what you've never had, you never miss". Why should it be any more impossible than the vast array of substitutes we've managed to produce? Further, let me point out that your word "impossible" doesn't mean impossible at all—it merely means that the thing hasn't happened yet.'

Mark let the argument drop. He felt that it contained a sufficient number of weak links for him to split later. At present he was more interested in the sights about him. He required more information on the 'natives'.

'We don't see a lot of them,' Gordon admitted. 'They get sick of us and our continual surface reminiscences, and tend to keep to themselves.'

'They don't even want to know about surface life?'

'Not much. Apart from their scarcely believing the tales, they find that they have no bearing whatever on their life down here, and don't help them at all. A lot of the prisoners go half crazy after a few years, and live in a permanent state of melancholia which both puzzles and frightens the "natives". They're happier on the whole when they're not mixing with us. Just as well.'

'And they don't want to escape?'

'Not a bit. And it would be a poor day for most of them if they did—more than likely they'd have agoraphobia pretty badly if they couldn't look up and see rock all round them.'

By now they had reached the far end of the cavern. Its occupants, for the most part, paid little more attention to Mark than a stare as he passed. His surprise that they did not come flocking round to ask questions grew less when he remembered that Smith, Gordon, and Mahmud must have circulated all his news of any interest. Turning and looking back on the listless crowd, he asked:

'Is this all they do? Just hang about?'

'A few of the melancholics, but most of them take an occasional turn in the fungus caves. Does them good to work, cheers them up a bit—trouble is that not enough work's needed, so for the most part they just sit and brood, or sleep. About the only excitement they get is a fight now and then over one of the women.'

'But can't they be put on to making something?'

'What? Oh, you mean furniture or stuff like that. I should think they could, but you see there's no wood. Some of them do a bit of carving in stone. I'll show you.'

He led the way into a tunnel ten feet or so in height. After fifty yards of it he paused at a side turning and called:

'Zickle!'

A tall, well-built Negro came out of the smaller passage. He grinned at them both in a friendly fashion.

'Hullo, Zickle! I've brought Mr. Sunnet to have a look at your work.' The Negro grinned even more broadly, and beckoned them in. 'Zickle was brought up at a mission school,' Gordon explained. 'Hence his choice of a name, but the training seems to have been a bit superficial, as you'll see.'

They entered a rock chamber of about the same size as Mark's sick-room. But the walls of it, instead of being painted, were elaborately carved. Mark at first sight felt bewildered. Zickle continued to grin.

'Here is the *pièce de résistance,*' Gordon said, turning to the left-hand wall. 'What do you make of that?'

Mark examined it carefully. In the centre was an oddly conventionalised figure of a man, hanging upon an undoubted cross. But it was not the plain cross of tradition; curious symbolism and alien conceptions had been carved into it until it bore more resemblance to a totem pole. Above the head of the crucified man leered a face of most horrifying hideousness.

The Negro saw Mark recoil as he looked at it.

'Him scare devils,' he explained.

'It ought to scare anything,' agreed Gordon cheerfully. 'Come closer, Mark, and have a look at the detail.'

He obeyed, and began to examine the workmanship with a manifest admiration which delighted Zickle. He turned back to stare at the tall, black figure.

'You did all this?' He waved a comprehensive hand.

'Yes, sir. I done him all.'

Mark turned back. The Negro might have few words to express himself, but the carving came from the brain of a man of unlimited ideas. He began to feel a little awed. The ingenuity with which Christianity and paganism had been welded together—he felt that a study of the work might give a new conception of both. Nor was the technique itself a mere following of tradition. There was a single mode of thought running through the whole bas-relief, but it was the product of an experimenting mind, unafraid to attempt effects which sometimes failed, but more often succeeded brilliantly.

'It's genius,' Mark said.

'You're right,' Gordon agreed. 'I've seen a lot of African sculpture, wood and stone, but nothing to touch this. It *is* genius—and the world will never see it. . . .'

'How long did it take to do all this?'

'Don't know. Zickle hasn't the slightest idea how long he has been in here. All I can tell you is that it was about a quarter done seven years ago, and has been complete for the last three. He carves most of the time when he isn't doing other work. Reckons it keeps him sane.' Gordon stared for a moment at the horrific head above the cross. 'I should say he's right—it must be better to get ideas like that out of the system.'

The Negro had been busy in another corner of the room. Presently he returned holding out a cup of polished stone to each of them. As they took them he pointed to some low stools carved carefully from stone, though in a fashion intended for wood. Gordon sat down and drank half his cupful at a gulp. Mark attempted the same, but the coarseness of the spirit set him coughing.

'My God, what is it?' he managed, at last.

'Stuff made from some of the fungi—it's an acquired taste.'

'So I should think.' Mark took a more careful sip.

Again he let his eyes wander over the carved walls, noticing and renoticing details. Below the cross, and separated from it by a broad horizontal band, he observed a panel which he had hitherto overlooked. It represented a number of squat, recognisable figures worked into a design among giant fungi.

'The white pygmies?' he inquired.

'Or demons—they're all the same to Zickle. He's convinced that this place is Hell.'

Zickle's face momentarily lost its grin, and he nodded.

'This very bad place—Hell. Plenty devils. Me plenty sins.'

'P'raps you're right; you know more about your own sins than I do.'

A voice came from the outside passage.

'Zickle there?'

The Negro and Gordon looked at one another for a moment; Gordon nodded, and Zickle called back. A man, a stranger to Mark, came slouching into the cave, followed by two companions. Like Smith he wore the dilapidated remnants of a French uniform, but there was little other resemblance. He was sallow skinned, with hair and beard as unkempt as the other's, but black. He nodded condescendingly to Gordon and turned to Zickle. The black faced him with an unamiable expression.

'Got a drink for me too?' The voice was harsh, and the words, though they came easily enough, were heavily accented.

Zickle hesitated. There was a murderous glare in his eyes. Gordon put his hand restrainingly on the black arm, and murmured something inaudible. The Negro nodded sullenly, and went in search of a cup with a bad grace. The newcomer laughed.

'Great little peacemaker, aren't you, Gordon?'

He took a good draught, wiped his lips on the back of his hand and looked at Mark with more contempt than curiosity.

'So this is the latest? And came in a plane, of all things.'

Gordon turned pointedly to Mark.

'This is Miguel Salvades. One would not like to say why he joined the Foreign Legion, but it might be guessed.'

Miguel laughed unpleasantly.

'I joined it because I killed a man at home—and I'm not above killing another.' He looked meaningly at the Negro. 'You can remember that. . . . What's his name?' he added, turning back to Gordon.

'My name is Mark Sunnet,' said Mark, angrily resentful at his third-party treatment. But Miguel continued to address himself to Gordon.

'Showing him the ropes?'

'Yes.'

'Guess you find it interesting. What've you seen?'

The last question was directed at Mark with a goodwill in such contrast with the man's earlier uncouthness that he was taken by surprise.

'Not much yet—only the big cave near here.'

'And this chamber of horrors. Well, you've got plenty more to see, hasn't he, Gordon?'

'Yes.' Gordon was not encouraging.

'The fungus caves and the water caves?'

'Yes.'

'And other things?'

'Yes.'

Miguel turned back to Mark. 'Yes, there's a lot of this for you to see yet. A lot more than you and most of us think. There's a lot I've not seen, but I'm going to.' He looked at Gordon as he spoke the last phrase, but the older man's face remained expressionless. Miguel grinned sardonically and tossed off the remains of his spirit.

'Come on, boys,' he said to his companions who had remained silently in the background. 'Let's go.'

He lounged out of the doorway, whistling. Mark and Gordon followed a few minutes later.

'What was all that about?' Mark asked curiously, as they recrossed the large cave.

Gordon chose to be evasive. 'Oh, you never can tell with Miguel. He likes his drink—probably thinks we've got a stock of it hidden away somewhere. Don't bother about him.'

Mark, unsatisfied, but perceiving his inquiry to be unwelcome, changed the subject.

'From what you've said, I gather that this place falls into two classes—the prisoners, and the "natives" who don't mix with them?'

'And the pygmies. Don't forget them.'

'What! In this part?'

'A few dozens of them. I suppose they're criminals of some kind. Very few of us know anything about them. You'll have to ask Mahmud if you want to know more. Only he and Miguel and a few others have troubled to learn their language.'

'Three main divisions, then. Prisoners like ourselves, "natives" born here, and pygmy criminals. That's it?'

'Yes, except that there are subdivisions among the prisoners—but you'll find that out soon enough.'

They continued their way back to the painted cave in silence. Mark was reflecting on what he had seen and heard. This world below the world was proving more complicated than he had expected, and, to judge from Miguel's behaviour, there was more activity than there would appear to be. His reverie was broken by a flood of excited speech which greeted their arrival at the doorway.

'Say, come in for an earful,' called Smith's voice above the rest. 'Mahmud's been getting the low-down.'

CHAPTER III

THE cave held, in addition to Smith and Mahmud, four strangers. Mark noticed that they turned to look at him with an interest which rather surprised him. The scrutiny, however, was brief, for they looked back expectantly to Mahmud. Smith spoke, forestalling the Arab:

'It ought to be easier for you guys to get this if you hear Mark's yarn first. Mark, give it 'em from the time you fell in, till you moored your *Sun Bird*.'

Mark obediently retold of the whirlpool, the fall, the

drifting through caves and passages, and the final landing in the lighted cave.

'Thanks,' Smith said at the end. 'Now, Mahmud, it's your turn.'

Mahmud, it appeared, had been over to have a talk with the pygmy prisoners. It was one of his habits to do this at fairly frequent intervals. He had mastered their language without any great difficulty, and could now speak it fluently. For several reasons, not very clearly perceived even by themselves, he and Smith felt that an understanding with the outcasts might possibly be of some advantage. In any case, it could do no harm to have knowledge of the happenings in the pygmies' own caves. On this occasion he had gone with an idea of finding out what Miguel was doing, for the latter's increasing intimacy with the little men had been causing some speculation. When he had arrived there, it was to find a state of excitement which had immediately diverted his interest.

There had been a recent addition to the band of pygmy criminals, and he had brought disturbing news with him. They had all been aware, though without a definite source of information, that things were not all well in the main caves, but now for the first time those in the prison caves got direct news.

'It's the water,' Mahmud explained excitedly. 'The New Sea is breaking through—though of course they don't know it is the New Sea.'

'Well, we learnt that from Mark,' Gordon observed.

'Yes, but that was only one break—it has come through in many. There have been several big falls like that, and a lot of smaller ones, too. Sometimes the bed of the New Sea gives way, but more often it comes in through the air shafts. That is not so bad; the water comes first in a trickle, and the shaft can usually be stopped before it gets serious. But in the big falls it *is* serious. So far they have managed to stop them by breaking the tunnels, but a lot of water has got in.'

Mark recalled the resounding crash in the tunnel through which he and Margaret had been swept to the lighted cave. So it was the pygmies who had caused that tunnel to collapse.... Mahmud was going on:

'They're scared. It is one thing to block tunnels, but

another to get rid of the water. Pumps could do it, but of course they have no pumps. In some places they have been able to make holes and drain it away to the lowest levels where it doesn't matter much, but that means that there's no room to get rid of the next lot. Besides, it's salt—it's got into some of the reservoir caves already, and joined the fresh-water streams. If the sea were to stay at its present level, they might win through all right, but the water is still rising outside, and there may be fresh breaks at any moment. They're very frightened.'

'Hey, steady there. How do they know the sea's still rising? None of them has ever showed his nose up there,' Smith interrupted.

'Because it keeps on coming in through more of those ventilating cracks as it reaches them.'

'What else are they doing?'

'Nothing much, from what I could hear. After all, what can they do? There seems to have been some talk of clearing off northward; there are caves at a higher level there, but they've been neglected so long that the fungus beds are no good. They might be able to replant them, but they're doubtful how long it will be before they yield.'

'So what it comes to,' said Smith reflectively, 'is a choice between staying here to drown, and going north to starve—unless, of course they take to the open. And they won't do that,' he added, looking questioningly at Gordon.

The latter shook his head. 'No, they won't do that,' he agreed.

'Why not?' asked Mark. 'Surely it's the reasonable thing to do?'

'Reason doesn't count much. Reason suggests that it is foolish to live on the side of a volcano, yet people continue to do it. These pygmies have been here too long, they've adapted too far. For one thing, the light outside would blind them right away. But the point is, whatever they do we're sure to be left behind. Pleasant outlook.'

Smith nodded. 'It only wants the water to break in here, and we'd drown like rats. There's just that one way for it to get out, and that's a hundred feet up—most of the caves aren't as high as that. Maybe we could swim until our heads hit the roof, then—good-bye——'

All the men in the room were silent for a while. Mark,

looking along the row of faces, saw that most of them had their eyes on the American. When at last one of the strangers said:

'What shall we do?' it was as though he spoke for all. A tacit admission of Smith's leadership. There might be sense in some of Gordon's theories, and, Mark learned later, much worth in many of his plans; Mahmud they knew to be subtle, excellent for intelligence work. But when action was needed, decisions were to be made, they looked to Smith. And he sat thinking...

Gordon watched him in the manner of one who could make a suggestion if called upon, but would not do so gratuitously. The stranger who had been the last to speak broke the silence again:

'If we double the work?' He suggested. 'It can't be far now——' He broke off suddenly and darted a suspicious glance at Mark. Smith looked up.

'You're too free with your trap, Braddon. Keep it shut closer.' He turned to look at Mark thoughtfully.

'That's all right,' Gordon broke in. 'He'll be with us all right. He's not one of Miguel's sort.'

'He wouldn't be here now if I thought he was,' Smith replied, 'but we've got to be careful all the same.' He addressed Mark directly. 'What we say goes no farther, not an inch—get that? It's not only Miguel we're up against, he's obvious, but some of his pals ain't. Keep this under your hat or—well, you won't have any place to wear a hat.'

'We've just seen Miguel,' Gordon broke in again.

'Where?'

'Zickle's place.'

'And what was he after?'

Gordon shrugged. 'Just prowling around to see what he could pick up—the only thing he got was a drink.'

'Well, let's hope he goes there again. Zickle might hand him some news.'

'What do you mean?'

'Miguel's after something, and if we want a false trail laid Zickle will do it. He hates Miguel like hell, but he's taking his time. I wouldn't like to be in Miguel's shoes when that nigger gets going.'

'I didn't know that,' said the man who had been

addressed as Braddon, in an aggrieved voice. 'What's it all about?'

Smith admitted to being not quite clear on the point himself. There had been something about the woman whom Zickle had lived with—Miguel's being mixed up in it left it pretty easy to guess the rest. Anyway, it was a more than ordinary hate.

'Miguel's going to get no change out of Zickle,' he added.

'But he's damned suspicious—he knows there's something in the air.'

'Well, don't we all?'

'No, I don't mean about the floods—you can bet he knows that all right. I mean about us.'

'Oh?' Smith turned to Mahmud. 'You heard anything about this?'

Mahmud was vague. Miguel, he admitted, had become much thicker with certain of the pygmy prisoners lately. There was more than mere curiosity behind the way he had taken to continual questioning.

'Try to get a line on it. It's up to you to find out what his game is. He must have some reason for nosing round the way he does—and that's reason enough for our keeping extra quiet. We've got to be careful.'

'Sure,' one of the others agreed impatiently, 'but what are we going to *do*?'

'Push on all work with the upward tunnel—hard as we can. What do you think about Greek's tunnel, Gordon?'

Gordon seemed to have thought the matter over already, and had his answer pat.

'Drop it.'

Smith considered. The upward tunnel climbed at a steep angle; it was hard to believe that its end could be far off the surface now. For an unknown number of years men had toiled at that tunnel. Nobody now living in the prison caves could remember when it had been started, and only a chosen few knew of its existence. A group of men determined not to perish easily in these catacombs had begun to hew their way out. Slowly, for their tools were miserable and inadequate, they had driven a passage up on as steep a slant as they could use. Progress had proved even slower than they had expected, and the way longer than they had thought; but they had been men of active brains and bodies. They continued their tunnel because they had begun it, and because it had given them hope and occupation. Without work they would have sunk to the level of most of the prisoners, minds and bodies would have deteriorated together to leave a hopeless apathy if not insanity. And so, through unnumbered years, the tunnel had gone on. As it had grown in length, so they had grown in age. They were no longer the strong young men of the caves. They became middle-aged, elderly, shorter in the breath, weaker in the arm.

But others had come along to replace them. Men of various races filtering into the caves through a score of unknown entrances, some enraged, some fatalistic, most of them destined to sink into lassitude, but always here and there a few whose strength of mind, whose will to live, drove them into activity. From these the planners of the tunnel had selected their successors: shown them the passage which would one day lead to sunlight and freedom, taught them how to work the rock and bade them get on with it. And the younger men had taken the worn-down chisels, and gone to work. Like the old men, they started to carve a road to liberty, and, again like the old men, they went on working to preserve sanity. Hopes became all but forlorn. Their tunnel was now several hours journey in length. They worked steadily, but the fire had gone. The light of expectation had dimmed from their eyes. Yet there was the sure knowledge that some day much come a hollow ringing in the rock, then a chisel point would break through to let in a gleam of daylight. And they plodded on.

They, too, grew old and were replaced by younger men. The authors of the tunnel would not now live to see daylight again; many were already dead, and those who were left, sunk in senility. But their work still lived; others toiled on with a faith which could be dimmed but not snuffed. The workers had chosen their successors well. Backsliders had been few. They had held themselves for the most part aloof from the discouraged, lest they might be contaminated. The rest knew, as of course they must, that the workers were active upon some plan, but they were not interested. If men liked to work when there was no call to perform any task more serious than an occasional spell in the fungus caves, it was their own foolishness. Moreover, the workers took good care to discourage such sporadic outbursts of curiosity as did occur.

With a few individualists such as Miguel, a problem was presented. They were unstable or unsocial characters. The workers knew that they could not be depended upon for regular work, yet they managed to keep their minds free of the sluggish acquiescence which engulfed the rest. They were misfits and, as such, undesirables; they were ignored as far as possible.

Among the workers themselves things had not always proceeded with complete smoothness. Twice there had arisen major differences of opinion. Some years before Smith's arrival, a man named Jameson had caused a split in the party by announcing his conviction that the present methods were, if not useless, at least far too laborious. Why not, he asked, drive a horizontal tunnel? It would be bound before long to connect with one of the pygmy caves, and then they could fight their way out. There were enough of them to overcome a whole army of dwarfs.

He was permitted, after some dissension to start his horizontal tunnel, but after fifty yards had encountered an underground river which rendered farther progress out of the question—his suggestion of trying again elsewhere met with no support.

Still another passage had been begun by a Greek whose name no one remembered. From an unknown source he had obtained information that another series of caverns was situated below the prison system at no great depth. He, like Jameson, was convinced that once in the main caverns they would have little difficulty in fighting their way to the surface. His downward passage had been extended by his followers to a depth of over two hundred feet without result, but was still regarded by some as having possibility of ultimate success. It was against this Greek's Tunnel, as it was called, that Gordon had unhesitatingly advised.

'Why?' Smith asked.

'For one thing I haven't much faith in it, but the real reason is that it's noisy. If we go on working there, and

Miguel's spying round in earnest, he'll find it sooner or later.'

'Does it matter much? After all, the up passage is the main thing. I was thinking that if we can get it through, it might act as a kind of drain in case we do get flooded.'

'There's something in that,' Gordon admitted. 'But I've got a feeling that it's better not to let Miguel know anything—he must have a pretty good reason for wanting to learn.'

'Well, that's simple enough,' suggested one of the others. 'Why not just bump him off?'

'It's not so easy. He's got pals. Besides, you can't tell how the rest would take it—or the "natives". Two can play at bumping off. We don't want our hands full with a vendetta just when we've decided to push the work on. No, the best thing is to work like hell on the up passage, there'll be no noise from that. We must be nearly through by now.'

The men looked unimpressed by the last hope. Mark, watching their faces, wondered how often they and others before them had heard those same words—'we must be nearly through.' Perhaps they had begun to doubt that the phrase could ever be true. Nevertheless, they accepted the suggestion of intensified work enthusiastically. It was as though a limit however indefinite, had been set. They were to work against time until they won or the floods came. It was a change from the weary monotony in which time counted for nothing. Smith rose to his feet.

'Come on, we'll tell the rest,' he said.

Mark, forgotten, watched them leave. Gordon turned back and thrust his head in through the doorway.

'You go to sleep for a while,' he directed. 'I'll show you round a bit more tomorrow. And if Miguel shows up here—though I don't suppose he will—not a word about the tunnels.'

He disappeared again, and there was a sound of quick steps as he hurried to catch up the others. Mark stretched out thankfully on his couch. He felt exhausted, and the activity had started the throbbing in his head again. He was not yet as strong as he had thought, it seemed. He began to drift sleepward with a better serenity, due partly to weariness, but more to wakened hopes of escape.

It had been good to hear Gordon's slip of the tongue. His 'tomorrow' had given a sense of hopeful future to this place of unending 'today'.

CHAPTER IV

'WHERE now?' Mark asked, as he and Gordon emerged once again into the large cavern.

'About time you saw the fungus caves—you'll have to put in your spell of work there later.' Gordon spoke in an unnecessarily loud voice which caused the members of several conversing groups to turn and look in their direction. One of the women pointed at Mark and laughed. Her voice held a jeering note which recalled a sudden memory of himself as a new boy at school being shown round by his housemaster. The words with which she followed the laugh were in a language unknown to him, but he could feel their implication. He had heard the same tones in the voices of practical men who condemned impractical idealists. It put him into the class of the self-righteous.

Yet there was nothing of self-righteousness about those of the 'workers' party he had met so far. They worked because they needed an outlet, and to keep sane, just as the Negro, Zickle, worked at his carving. Such superiority as they undoubtedly did maintain was incidental rather than intentional; the merely static condition of avoiding the mental rot which set in in the minds of the unoccupied. The attitude of the latter showed that they were not entirely unaware of their own deterioration though they had not considered it worth checking. Life in the caves offered the minimum of joys, why forgo them? The women particularly quailed at the thought of dying with the knowledge that they had never lived. It was more easy and more comprehensible to live within an established order than to attempt to change it. What, he wondered, would Margaret have done had she been condemned to this place? Would she tend to accept the customs of the majority as these women did, or would she fight...?

He tried once more to suppress the figure of her which was constantly slipping into his mind. Bad enough for her influence to be rising continually from his subconscious, but far worse when she slit the diaphragm between his selves and invaded his active thoughts. He endeavoured again to thrust her back by taking an active interest in his surroundings.

The way led this time past the turning to Zickle's cave and through a larger tunnel. Mark noticed that the prison caves like the rest were a mixture of nature and craft. The interconnecting passages had been enlarged often from mere cracks to eight or ten-foot tunnels, according to their importance. Awkward or dangerous corners were smoothed and trimmed. Before the roof lights were fixed, a clearance had been made of those massive slabs which in natural caverns hang aloft, ready, to all appearance, to crash upon the heads of the venturesome. Cracks in the ground had been filled up or bridged over. Stalactites had been ground away in order that their spikes might no longer hang like Damoclean swords. Fallen rocks, conical stalagmites, and all the litter which must once have rendered these places fantastic and awe-inspiring, were gone. The floors had been made as level as possible, the walls regularised, and disorderly nature tamed to a prison-like severity.

Gordon indicated various side openings as they passed. This, he said, led to a series of caves given over to the 'natives'; another to the pygmy prisoners' warren.

Mark gave up trying to memorise their route. He was aware of a constant succession of caves, passages, and side turnings, all as full of character for his guide as the streets of a town, but to a newcomer monotonously indistinguishable from one another. The men and women whom they met glanced at them with little interest and passed on with unhurried steps. He noticed that a number of them were bearing sections of the great fungi upon their backs.

Gordon stopped in a cavern slightly larger than the average, and waved his hand towards the end wall in the manner of a showman.

'There's a problem for you,' he said.

Mark advanced to examine more closely a line of

figures graven in low relief.

'The Egyptian gods?' he asked.

'Some of them, but others too. Look here.' He began pointing them out. 'Here's Hathor, with the cow's head—and this chap I think is Set, though the head's a bit different; shorter in the muzzle than usual—and, see, this must be meant for Ra; the hawk's head, all right, but they've missed out the sun's disc. And look at his sceptre, it's got a globe instead of a dog's head on it. . . . Mahmud says that the globe is symbolic of these.' He pointed up to the glowing lights. 'If so, it means that the carving was done after these people renounced the upper world and the sunlight. Ra was the creator, the giver of all things—without that light there could be no life down here. And what's this?' 'This' was a female figure upon which was mounted a fish in place of a head. 'Presumably a fertility goddess of some kind. There was a goddess Hamhit, but she had a fish on top of her head, not instead of it. And here's another chap with a serpent's head—now, if it were a uraeus. . . . But it's a plain, ordinary snake's head. Next to him is Bast, sistrum and all. . . .'

'Bast?' said Mark suddenly.

'Of course, look at the cat's head. The Greeks called her Bubastis later, and mixed her up; they made her preside over a lot of things she was never intended to. The Egyptians saw her as a gentle, warming influence, she was tied up somehow with Ra, but . . .'

But Mark was not listening. Bast—that damned cat. Could there be any connection? He remembered that Margaret had been holding the cat when they were attacked.

'The pygmies did these?' he asked, breaking in.

Gordon, knocked out of his vocal stride, looked puzzled. Mark repeated:

'Did the pygmies do these carvings?'

'Pretty certainly. Long ago, I should think, before these were used as prison caves. Why?'

'Do they still worship these gods?'

'I think so—or some very like them, according to Mahmud. Why?'

Mark ignored the second question as he had the first. The possibility of the cat's presence making any difference had never struck him until now. There had been no reason why it should before he had seen that cat-headed figure. Might not the fact that she was carrying it account for Margaret's non-appearance in the prison caves? He put the question to Gordon, who looked thoughtful.

'I wonder. It might be so. Of course,' he added, 'it's not absolutely certain that the pygmies carved these. There must have been Egyptians down here at some time—pure law of averages—but the carvings are sufficiently different in detail to convince me that they didn't do them. Ra, in particular, would never have been allowed to lack his disc of the sun. If prisoners had made them they would have tended to exaggerate the sun; it would have been the most potent symbol of the lot. So I think on the strength of that we are justified in assuming that the pygmies did do them. Moreover, Mahmud has talked about a kind of animal worship. Animals are so rare that when one does get in, it becomes deified automatically.'

'Then it is possible that Bast—our cat, I mean—is being worshipped?'

'Possibly, yes, but I wouldn't build on it. We don't really know much about them.'

Nevertheless, Mark did allow, even encouraged, his mind to build upon the unsteady foundation. If it were true that the ancient worship of Bast persisted here and that the cat remained her sacred symbol, what would Margaret's position be? Would she not be revered as a messenger of the goddess, divinely appointed to convey a token? Treated with honour, perhaps declared a demi-goddess? The misgivings which has closed about him grew tenuous and began to drift away. This, without any doubt, must be the explanation of her absence from the prison caves. . . .

Gordon watched him, and, seeing his face clear, knew the line his thoughts were taking. There was little to be gained from pulling down such a castle in the air, though for his own part he remained unconvinced of the girl's safety. It seemed every bit as likely that she might have been condemned as impious for handling a sacred object —and the crime of impiety usually involves penalties of the more unpleasant kinds. Still, that probability need not be broached. Mark was not yet fully recovered from his illness. The sense of hope would be a better medicine than any they could provide, so Gordon went on talking about the pygmies.

'They must have been much more numerous in the old days. They're dwindling now, like all the primitive races, and the whole system of caves is far larger than they need. I have thought that those carvings were probably made when the population was dense, before they were able to abandon this system for use as a prison, but I may be wrong. They could have been made by pygmy prisoners in some effort at atonement. There's no telling. The only certainty is that the figures are like, and yet unlike their Egyptian counterparts.'

Mark came down to earth.

'But it's odd that they should have adopted and kept the Egyptian gods.'

'If they did.'

'But, surely——'

'I mean how do you know that the Egyptians did not adopt their gods, or that the two sets did not spring from some common source. This pygmy race is old, I fancy—older than you have any conception. The ancient Egyptians are moderns compared with our pygmies.'

'How do you make that out? The system of caves, of course, must have taken centuries to perfect, but still to say that they are older than the Egyptians...?'

Gordon shrugged. 'I'll give you my reasoning sometime, but it is a long explanation. We must get on now.'

He led from the cave of the carvings into a gently descending tunnel, and before long Mark became aware that the silence about them was no longer complete. There grew at first a mere agitation of murmurous echoes, indefinite and hard to place, but a new sound, different from the confused shuffle of occasional feet and voices. It grew clearer as they proceeded, clarifying gradually from one composite disturbance until the splash of trickling water became audible against the background of its gurgling passage.

They paused at the spot where a small stream gushed from a crack in the wall. Gordon picked up a stone bowl and held it under the flow. He drank thankfully.

'It's a blessing the salt hasn't got into our water yet,' he said relievedly. 'That'd be worse than drowning.'

He went on morbidly to elaborate the horrors which would attend lack of fresh water, but even the picture he drew of the prisoners driven crazy by thirst failed to subdue the elation which had risen in Mark.

By this time he had contrived out of a few straws of suggestion to build a raft of remarkable buoyancy. A feeling of hope had come flooding in to change every mental process. His spirits had stirred out of lethargy. It was as if weakness and worry had created a rust in him; now that rust was all washed away, and there was fresh oil on the bearings. He felt that his body would be able to break out of this prison even as his mind had. Gordon was astonished at the transformation. He looked almost a stranger, and one who walked with a springy step rare among the cave dwellers. He was silently astonished at the control the mental was showing over the physical.

A faint, familiar odour and a dampness became noticeable, and Mark knew that they must be nearing the fungus caves. There were five of them, interconnected, Gordon had told him, of which the combined acreage had easily supplied their needs until lately, but with the increase of population, both by new arrivals and births, the margin had been narrowed. All the conditions of life in this underground world, it seemed, were hastening concurrently to crisis.

Gordon stooped suddenly, and held up his hand. Mark could hear nothing but the faint murmur of the stream as it flowed beside them.

'Someone running,' Gordon said.

He grasped Mark's arm, and drew him back against the wall, puzzled and silent. Mark had not been long enough in the caves to realise that something unusual must be afoot. For a man to run here was all but unknown. Why should he? In this place time could neither be lost nor gained: it did not exist. Now he began to distinguish the sound of footsteps which would soon overtake them. Both watched the last corner expectantly. The sound grew louder.

'Only one,' said Gordon. He bent down to pick up a piece of rock, settling it firmly in his hand.

A form clad in flowing, grey tatters rounded the corner.

It came on until it caught sight of them, flattened against the wall. It stopped abruptly. Gordon dropped his stone, and stepped out.

'Mahmud!' He called in surprise.

The Arab approached, somewhat out of breath.

'What is it?' Gordon asked, joining him. The three walked on together.

'Miguel,' explained Mahmud excitedly. 'I've been talking to the pygmies; I found some of them who hate him, and I got it from them.'

'Well, what was it?' Gordon was impatient.

'Miguel's trying to find out where the tunnel is.'

'We knew that—what else could he have been trying to find out?'

'But there's more than that. He's got several of his friends and most of the pygmy prisoners behind him, and they've been bargaining with the pygmies outside. Miguel offered to show them our tunnel in exchange for his freedom, but they didn't like that, so he compromised. He would show them the tunnel if they would take him out of the prison system and give him the run of the ordinary caves.'

'That wouldn't do him much good.'

'He and his friends think it would—they've probably got an idea of his getting out somehow, and bringing help. Anyhow, the bargain's been made.'

Gordon stared. 'It has?'

'It has.'

'So that's what he's been up to, is it? He's a fool if he thinks they'll ever give him a chance of getting right outside.'

'But he's got some scheme—you can be sure of that.'

'Does he know yet where the passage is?'

'No, but——'

'With an incentive like that it won't take him long to find out, eh?'

The Arab nodded.

'Then he'll have to be dealt with,' Gordon went on.

'You mean, kill him?' Mark asked.

'I do—he's a rat.'

'But his friends—won't they take up the bargain?'

'We can treat all traitors alike.'

'And how far will that get you? As I see it, the real damage is done already—the pygmies know that the tunnel exists. It was only really safe while it remained unknown to them. The cat's out of the bag now, and I don't see that killing Miguel's going to do much good.'

'It he's not found the tunnel yet, it might. He's a long way the brightest of that gang. It'd set them back and give us more time. If he has found it, he must be got rid of at once before he can tell anyone else.'

'You won't be sure he hasn't told.'

'Sure enough. Miguel's kind keeps everything up its sleeve as long as it safely can. He'd be scared of the rest letting him down if he told them anything until the last moment.'

Gordon was still talking as they came to the first of the fungus caves, and Mark found himself almost as surprised as he had been when he saw the giant mushrooms in the outer caves. His memory had reduced their size, and despite his expectations, he was taken aback. He would have liked to linger and examine the fantastic picture they made, but his companions were in too great a hurry. Gordon led round to the right, keeping to the strip of open space, between the growths and the wall, where walking was easy. At no great distance they encountered a passage only a few yards long, and passed through it into another cave. Here, the scene was more open for much of the fungus had been cut away to be carried to the living caves where it would be rendered more easily edible by mashing or other processes. They crossed the loam, littered with chips and stubs of felled fungi, to plunge into the still standing growths beyond. The going became slower and more awkward. Gordon warned Mark to step over the twining ground tendrils, and if possible to avoid bruising them. Not, he admitted, that there was any great need for care as yet, but it would be better not to leave a trail.

It was in the third fungus cave that he became really wary. He led a complicated path among the trunks and marrow-like objects, zigzagging and doubling continually. Mark did his best to imitate the skill which both he and the Arab showed in passing without trace, but he felt that he was making a poor job of it. He was responsible for a number of broken stalks and crushed tendrils, however, they were scattered, and it seemed unlikely that anyone could follow so tortuous a trail from so few clues. He realised at last why Gordon had used loud tones to announce that they were going to the fungus caves. They were an obvious sight for a newcomer, but somewhere hidden away among them was the beginning of the upward tunnel.

He was relieved when he could see, between the mushroom heads, the grey stone wall only a few yards ahead. A minute or two more, and they stood on the fringe of the vegetation.

The sound of a sudden scuffle caused them all three to turn sharply. Mark had a glimpse of a man who ran from the wall and disappeared between the trunks to their right. Mahmud, too, saw him. Before the full significance came home to the others, he was in swift, silent pursuit, with the rags of his burnous streaming behind him. Mark opened his mouth, but Gordon raised his hand. The two stood listening.

Mahmud vanished among the stalks by the track which the other had left. For some moments there was nothing to be heard but the thudding of feet, mingled with the muffled snapping of stalks and tentacles. The fugitive was blundering blindly ahead, trampling the lower fungi underfoot, and turning aside only for the thicker trunks. The slender stalks which he swept from his way, broke, not with sharp crack of branches, but dully, like rotten wood. The watchers could follow his trail by the way in which more than one tall, umbrella-like head shook and leaned to subside slowly into the lower growths. A cloud of white spores broke suddenly into the air; they could hear Mahmud splutter and cough as he came to them. A minute later followed a choked cry; a tremendous agitation and threshing amid the trembling stalks. Mahmud and the fugitive had come to grips.

'Come on,' Gordon said, starting towards the sound.

'Look,' called Mark, but the other did not hear. He was already away. Mark alone had seen another figure break from the hiding of a mushroom trunk, and speed away up the clear space beside the wall. He gave chase.

The second fugitive was wiser than the first. He had no

intention of tangling himself in stalks; he was depending on speed and a start of thirty yards to carry him safely to an opening.

Mark pounded along. He was in poor form for violent exercise, and saw that he was barely holding his own. The man ahead glanced over his shoulder, and then put on a spurt. Mark tried desperately to increase his own speed, but his feet felt clumsy and heavy. He scarcely knew why this man must be caught, but the attitude of the others had shown it to be vital. The man had begun to slacken—such violent exercise was not encouraged by life in the caves. But his own rate, too, was falling off, and his heart thumping painfully; he tried desperately to force his lagging feet.

A pale, fat tentacle defeated him. It had grown out more adventurously than the rest. Mark's descending boot crushed it into a slibbery mess, and he pitched head first into the loam.

He sat up at once, brushing the dirt from his eyes, but the fugitive had gone, and he himself was too winded to continue. He remained where he was for some minutes recovering, before he rose to walk back to the others.

He found them in a trampled arena. Mahmud lay on the ground, breathing heavily. Across the other side Gordon was bending over a still form with a queerly twisted head. As Mark approached, he straightened up.

'Damn,' he muttered, 'we might have learned something. What did you want to kill him for?'

'His neck or mine,' panted the Arab.

'There was another,' Mark said, sitting down wearily.

'The devil there was. Where is he?'

Mark explained.

'Damnation. You couldn't tell who he was?'

'I'd never seen him before.'

'Wish I'd seen him—blast it! Sure to have been one of Miguel's lot—this chap is. That means that we've got to get busy. Come on, Mahmud.'

The Arab rose unsteadily, still breathing hard.

'Come on,' Gordon repeated to Mark.

They followed him back to the fringe of the plantation. Gordon, without hesitation, went up to the wall and inserted all his fingers in an irregular crack. He leaned back, and slightly to the right, with all his weight. A rocky slab before him followed, pivoting slowly. He hustled the two through the space behind it and laid hold of the edge to drag it back into place.

Mark found himself in a chamber which contained nine or ten men. Among them he recognised one of the party who had visited Smith, and also the Negro, Zickle; the rest were strangers. A small globe in the roof shone dimly, but enough to show in the opposite wall, the beginning of a narrow passage leading upward at a severe angle. Gordon wasted no time.

'Miguel's on to us,' he said.

The Negro bared his teeth unpleasantly, otherwise the response was disappointing.

'Well, what about it?' asked one of the men. 'He can't do much, and we can croak him if he gets rough.'

'Not so simple,' said Gordon. 'Go on, Mahmud; tell them about it.'

Mahmud gave once more his report of Miguel's pact with the pygmies.

Some of the faces in the group began to look serious; others, including that of the one who had suggested 'croaking' Miguel, remained unimpressed. From the latter's next remark, it became obvious that he had not grasped the situation.

'There aren't so many pygmy prisoners. They can't give us much trouble.'

Mahmud explained afresh:

'It's not only the prisoners—he's made a pact with the pygmies in the outer caves.'

'How? They never come in here.'

'I don't know how the pact was made—I only know that it was. If he helps them to stop our tunnelling, he gets the run of the outer caves. Don't you see?'

'But how are they going to stop us. They never come——'

'Damn it, man,' Gordon broke in. 'Use your brains. I know we've never seen the pygmies in here except as prisoners—but they can invade us any time they like. We're not strong—a hundred and fifty at most. They'll have Miguel and his lot, most of the pgymy prisoners and the "natives" with them. The rest of the prisoners we can't be sure about. They may join up for the sake of a bit of excitement, but I think most of them will be neutral. Anyhow, we'd better be ready for them. Where's Smith?'

The other tilted his head towards the back of the cave. 'Up the tunnel.'

'At the end?'

'No. He hasn't been gone long.'

'Well, somebody go and fetch him—tell him it's urgent.'

One of the younger men scrambled to his feet and made for the entrance. Gordon looked over the group again.

'You, Zickle, get all our men you can find, and tell them to come here quick.' As the Negro rose, he added, 'And look out for Miguel—he might try an ambush.'

'Sure,' said Zickle. He seemed not unpleased by the prospect.

The stone door swung back after him, and the rest of the men faced Gordon expectantly. He started to speak, and then shook his head.

'No, better wait for Smith. This is more in his line.'

CHAPTER V

DURING the enforced wait a change crept over the group. Some of that lethargy which, despite all their efforts, had touched every one of them in greater or less degree, sloughed away. Time began to mean something. Even those who were sceptical of the real sciousness of Gordon's warning became more alert. Whether the danger were actual or not, here was an occurrence to create a moment of interest in the monotony. Apathy was broken by a fidgeting and shuffling which told of increasing tension. A few discussed the situation as far as they knew it. Their eyes brightened. The flaccidity of planless dreaming which had dulled each face disappeared as expressions became active. Mark marvelled at the change much as a short time ago Gordon had marvelled at a similar change in him.

He let his gaze roam round the stone chamber. It was a bare place, furnished only with benches and seats of hewn rock, and a few bowls containing water or fungus spirit. In one corner lay a few makeshift chisels, hammers, and other tools, among which he recognised long, thin French bayonets ground down by use. He wondered idly how the heavier tools had been acquired; iron and steel must be precious and rare in the caves. The accumulation of years, he supposed, collected from incoming prisoners. A problem occurred to him: how was the rubbish and detritus disposed of? Of the many tons of rock gouged out year after year, there was no sign, yet enough must have been removed to form a small mountain. He put the question to Gordon, who explained:

'Every now and then we come across fissures and faults into which the rubbish can be tipped. Some of them are narrow and not very deep, so that they are quickly filled up; others seem practically bottomless, and have to be bridged. We get across and continue the tunnel, sending the rubbish back to be dropped down the cleft behind until we strike another fault, then the same thing happens again.

'But in the beginning? when they made this place, for instance?'

Gordon shrugged.

'I suppose they had to carry it all away until the first fissure was struck. It must have been heavy work for the poor devils. I'm glad——'

A sudden scraping of the stone door interrupted him. He jumped up and seized a jagged piece of stone. The rest followed his example, standing with arms drawn back, ready to let fly. The door continued to turn ponderously upon its stone hinges. A streak of light from the fungus cavern appeared. The arms of the waiting men grew tense. A tousled, bearded head appeared; its owner grinned broadly at the sight of them.

'O.K. You can can your phoney pineapples,' he remarked cryptically. 'It's me and the boys.'

The threatening arms were lowered, and the held breaths released. The door swung wide enough to admit a man's body. The speaker entered, followed by ten or more companions of assorted races and nationalities.

'What's the big idea?' he demanded. 'That crazy nigger, Zickle's talkin' like the Day of Judgment's comin'. He gone nuts?'

'No, he's all right. We sent him. It's Miguel that's the trouble——'

'Trouble? What, that lousy wop? Gees, you ain't gotta get a whole bunch o' guys jest to beat him up. He's yeller; his whole gang's yeller. What's he been pullin', anyway?'

Gordon began to explain once more. Before he was halfway through, Smith came clattering out of the tunnel, demanding information. Mahmud was required to tell his tale for the third time.

Smith looked serious, and listened in silence. He frowned when Gordon completed the report by telling of the spies in the fungus caves.

'You're right,' he admitted. 'We've got to get busy. Mahmud's yarn mightn't have meant a lot by itself, nor might a couple of guys snoopin' around here. But the two together ... Well, it just means things are moving.' He turned to the latest comer. 'Is Zickle getting the rest, Ed?'

Ed looked doubtful, and scratched his beard.

'I guess he's doin' his best, but mostly they're razzin' him. Me and the boys thought there might be somethin' to it, so we came around.'

'Well, you and some of the boys better get right back and tell 'em to stop razzin' that nigger, or it'll be the last razzin' they'll do. Get me? Bring 'em here damn quick, and no maybe.'

'O.K., I getcha.'

The massive Ed and four of his followers went out, leaving the door open behind them. Smith resumed:

'Now, we've got to hustle. If Mahmud's right, the pygmies'll start to move just as soon as Miguel hands them the low down on this tunnel. The time we've got depends on how long it'll take them to get the news round and mobilise themselves. What we've got to do is to hold them off, and keep on working the tunnel. We've done a hell of a lot of work, and I'm damned if we're going to let it go for nothing now. It can't be much farther to the top—we might be through any time now. The point is, where'll we hold them?'

After discussion, the obvious course of blocking the main passages had to be abandoned, albeit reluctantly. There were, as Smith pointed out, too many side turnings for safety. The sprawling network of ways would, in spite of the greatest care, leave opportunities for flanking movements and rear attacks. There was, moreover, the possibility that the pygmies might dig downward from caves existing above, and outmanoeuvre the defenders in that way.

The safer course, although more onerous, would be to fight the battle nearer home. The fungus cave in which the tunnel entrance was situated could be reached only by three openings at the farther end, and it was Smith's plan to build a rampart across the narrowest part of the cavern. This, he pointed out, would secure for themselves about two-thirds of the place, and therefore an ample supply of food for some time. The rampart itself would be built from the growths on the other third, thereby denuding that part of cover for the attackers.

With the plan decided, he began to assign duties:

'Mahmud and two others to take the three tunnels and act as scouts. One man to go up and fetch all those who can be spared from the tunnelling—but don't let the work slack off. The rest to build the rampart.'

Mark was given a sharp-edged rock flake and instructed to fell giant fungi at the far end of the cave. Despite the unhandiness of such a tool, he found that he made good progress at first. The serrations cut saw-like into the soft fibre and pulp more easily than he had expected, and it was possible to topple the mushrooms over when one had cut little more than half-way through the stem. The great heads were wrenched loose from most as they fell; those which still adhered were worked off by leverage. Each white trunk was seized by two other men and rolled away, while Mark went on to the next.

But the work quickly became tedious; it was not long before his right arm began to ache with the effort of wielding the cutting stone. The men to either side of him were making better progress. Their muscles were in harder condition from their work in the tunnel; moreover, they were not recently off a sick bed; nevertheless, he continued with a desperate determination while the ache spread from his arm across his shoulders. He must, he thought, have laid low over twenty thick trunks before an interruption occurred.

A sudden hubbub down the narrow end of the cave caused all the men to pause in their hacking. Their hands changed the grip on their stones. They stared at the barrier of stems before them, ready to hurl the sharp flakes at the first pygmy form which should show. Somebody ahead, perhaps one of the scouts, anticipated them. There was the clatter of a stone against a rock wall. It was followed by the bellow of a familiar voice.

'Blast your eyes. It's me and the boys.'

The burly Ed came crashing his elephantine way among the stalks. He seemed to be rejoicing that it was no longer necessary for him to move traillessly. Smith called from behind, where he was superintending work on the barricade.

'Got 'em all, Ed?'

'O.K., the whole bunch. What do we do now?'

Mark thrust his cutting stone towards one of Ed's followers.

'You get on with it,' he suggested. 'I'm all in for the present.'

He walked back a little, and sat down to rest where he could watch the progress of barricade building. In places the wall was already several feet high, and difficulties in raising the fat, pulpy logs were increasing. For the first time he saw how handicapping a lack of wood may be. With poles for use as levers the trunks could have been handled easily. With planks they could have made a ramp up which to roll them. If the cutting flakes could have been set in hafts they would have been ten times more efficient. Even neolithic man, he thought bitterly, was better equipped with tools than they were, and as for weapons ... With wood they could have made spears, and, with the right kinds of wood, bows and arrows. There could have been clubs, both plain, and headed with stone. But without wood they were practically weaponless—bits of rock and fists....

The arrival of Ed and his reinforcements had given a great spurt to the work. The majority of the hundred and fifty which Smith had called 'workers' were now employed at clearing, rolling the trunks, and building the wall. The task promised to be shorter than Mark had expected. Smith had chosen the position well. The floor-plan of the cave was shaped roughly to a figure eight, of which the lower half was twice the size of the upper. At the waist the opposite walls approached within fifty yards of one another, and it was across this comparatively narrow space that he was erecting his defences. If they could succeed in clearing all the ground on the lesser side before the attack arrived, the pygmies would have the unpleasant task of crossing it without cover.

A short rest was enough to revive Mark considerably. He had not been exhausted, but suffering from the rebellion of muscles lately unused, and now put to a sudden strain. He rose and walked towards the barricade. Smith saw him from his supervising position on the top, and beckoned him up.

'Come and give these fellows a hand,' he directed.

On the defenders' side of the wall he found a group, including Gordon, industriously working with coarse cord. The cord itself had been made by plaiting narrow strips of the tougher fungus skins, and then shrinking them either by natural drying, or by careful smoking above a slow fire. He watched them carefully for a while. A conveniently shaped stone was selected, and a number of lengths of cord tied round it. The depending ends of the cords were gathered together and bound tightly for a distance of twelve or fourteen inches from the stone head. Another tight binding was then superimposed upon this. The result was a short club with a handle which, though by no means rigid, was not too flexible for use. The finished weapon, save for the bulging stone head, appeared not unlike one of those hanks in which clothes' line is sold. Mark picked one up, and swung it experimentally. The balance was poor, and the pliability made the stroke awkward. Nevertheless it could be nasty for close fighting; far nastier than a mere fist, or a stone held in the hand. He dropped it back among the dozen or so already completed, and sat down to do his share.

The barrier was all but complete. A white wall of stacked mushroom logs, twelve feet high, stretched from side to side of the cave with only one break of a couple of yards. The top of the wall was sloped down on the inner side to give cover for the defenders. The outer part had been faced with a buttress of the circular mushroom heads, ranged in rows like huge shields. Seen from the now almost bare end of the cave it resembled an immense testudo, or the carapace of a fabulously armoured beast. Smith strode through the remaining gap and turned to survey the work with satisfaction. It was doubtful whether the mushroom heads would long stay in position, but they certainly ought to defeat the first charge. It would be impossible even to attempt to climb the wall until those smoothly curving plaques had been removed.

Through the gap poured a continuous double stream of men, entering with burdens, and emerging empty handed to fetch more. Such fungi as were not required for actual building material were being hurried within, partly for use as food, and partly in pursuance of the plan to clear the ground. Only the lowest trailing growths were left; they would be useless for purposes of concealment, and might serve the secondary purpose of slowing up the attackers.

Smith waited anxiously while the last marrow-like object and the last giant puff-balls were carefully trundled away. The men had worked willingly and fast. It was so long since he had thought in terms of time that he was at a loss to estimate the number of hours which had passed since he had heard Mahmud's story, but it could scarcely be more than five, nor less than four. There was no telling when the pygmies would show up. Mentally he went through the steps which would be necessary.

Miguel, if indeed it was he who had been in the cave, must first get back to the pygmy prisoners; then word would be passed on to the outside pygmies *via* the guards at the only exit from the prison caves. There must be mobilisation—or were they already waiting? Then descent into this system, and finally the march throughout its length.... For the hundredth time he gave up the attempt to calculate how long all this would take. There were too many variables for the answer to be of the slightest use. The only certain thing was that they might arrive at any moment now....

He recalled Mahmud and the other scouts from the passages, and gave orders for the gap to be closed. A row of guards was posted, each with a supply of throwing stones, along the wall top. The more exhausted of the builders lay down to snatch some sleep, a few of the fresher were sent up to relieve the workers in the tunnel. Whatever happened, the tunnelling must continue. Ultimately, it was their only hope. The food they had could be made to last a long time, but it was more than doubtful whether they would be able to grow fresh at anything like the rate of consumption. A hundred and fifty men at work would get through a staggering amount of pulped mushrooms. The tunnel must be finished before the food gave out....

Such men, as were not under orders nor tired out, joined the group of weapon makers. Production was not only speeded up, but varied. The bulky Ed, having contrived for himself a kind of mace worthy of Goliath, turned his attention to primitive ballistics and produced a kind of bolas consisting of two stones linked by a double-plaited cord. Mark had some doubts whether this early ancestor of chain shot would prove of any worth in battle, but Ed had none. He gleefully practiced whirling it round his head, and letting fly with a fair accuracy. The supply of weapons was not complete when a shortage of cord became critical. Slow fires were started, and the manufacture of more begun. As this was a skilled job, Mark found himself without occupation. He sought a comfortable spot, and lay down, watching the rest.

It was hard to believe that the industrious men about him were the same who had been so apathetic a few hours ago. Strange how easily the zest for life could be diminished or revived. Those other prisoners back in the living caves were completely demoralised, and these had been little better. The need for action had worked in them like some miraculous tonic. They were laughing again; chatting as they plaited the cords. The weight of depression had been lifted, and the true men released.

Mark's head dropped lower. The chatter and laughter became a murmurously pleasant confusion. His eyelids drooped wearily, and he slid from half sleep into true sleep.

CHAPTER VI

HE awoke and sat up simultaneously, with a sudden, severe pain in the shin.

'What the hell——?' he began, putting a hand to the injured part.

The man who had tripped over him was struggling to his feet again. He spoke wheezily, for he was part winded:

'They're coming. Get to it.'

The sense of being hardly done by vanished. Mark jumped up, snatched the corded club which lay beside him, and ran for the wall. Scrambling up the protruding trunk ends, he flung himself flat on the top.

Only then did he come fully awake and realise that no battle was in progress. He raised his head cautiously to peer over the edge. The cleared space was as empty as were the cave mouths behind it. He began to grow indignant at being thus stampeded to no purpose, but a glance about served to reassure him. There was a bustling activity among the defenders; the wall was being manned in a business-like way. He turned to the next man:

'Where are they?'

His neighbour did not understand. He shook a dark complexioned, Italian-looking head, and muttered an unintelligibility. The man beyond him spoke up.

'They're coming, all right. They were so long on the way that Smith got worried. He sent out Mahmud to see what was up, and they nearly got him. He's just back.'

'Many of them?' Mark inquired.

'Can't tell. He just saw the leaders coming along the passage, and ran for it.'

The hubbub of the defenders was quieting. Smith's voice still rose occasionally in sharp orders, but by now most of the men were at their stations. With the passing of the first flurry of excitement an expectant tenseness grew. Word came down the line. No one was to act till Smith gave the word. It went the length and the last whispering echoes of repeating voices died away into a silence broken only by deep drawn breaths. All ears were strained to catch the first faint sounds of approach.

Mark's attention wandered. It came to him in a flash that by joining the 'workers' he had cut himself farther off from Margaret than ever. He had managed on the slenderest evidence to convince himself that she was still alive and prisoner in the outer caves. Until now he had been merely one of the inhabitants of the prison caves, but by joining Smith he had put himself into a prison within a prison. Suppose he had joined Miguel's band? He might have got the run of the outer caves, and some chance of finding her. But wasn't it possible that the pygmies were double-crossing Miguel? It seemed more than likely. After all, once they had destroyed the weak spot which the tunnel made in the prison system, why should they trouble themselves about Miguel any longer?

It became clear that not only the fate of all of them, but of Margaret as well, depended upon the success of the tunnel. If they could only hold out until the surface was reached, it would mean the end of the pygmies. Once they were in touch with civilisation there would be no difficulty in collecting an expedition to rescue the remaining prisoners and to round up the whole unsuspected nation of troglodytes. Perhaps he had taken the wiser course after all. Rescue for Margaret could only come from the outside. Even if he had the luck to get into the outer cave system and to find her, what then? They could scarcely hope to make the upper world unassisted.

And what were they doing to Margaret? Why were they keeping her there? They'd never kept anyone before. It must be that damned cat—why else?

A stir ran through the line of men on the wall. Were they coming at last? Mark strained to hear. Yes, the whisper of a shuffle. The froning of naked feet on the stone floor. Thoughts of Margaret vanished. His hand, like those of the men to left and right of him, went out to grasp a throwing stone. He kept his eyes to the crack between the trunks forming the topmost rampart; it gave him a view of the main opening and one of the subsidiaries. Simultaneously, white, monkey-like forms became visible in both.

One of the reasons for delay became apparent. The intention had been to trap them in this cave. The two companies (and probably a third, out of his sight) had been timed to arrive together. There was to be no dodging out through one hole while the pygmies came in by another. The complexion of the affair became slightly altered. The move showed that the pygmy programme comprised not only destruction of the tunnel, but the punishment of those who had made it.

But now it was the pygmies own turn to be surprised. He saw them halt and gesticulate in amazement towards the barrier. Those behind thrust forward, crowding the leaders into the cavern. A chatter of high-pitched voices became audible.

It came to Mark with surprise that this was only his second meeting with the little people. He had heard so much of them, and thought of them so frequently, that he had come to think of them as a familiar sight, though he had seen none since his original encounter in the outer caverns. The odd feeling that he had seen the type before struck him again. He had meant to tell Gordon of this half recognition, but it had slipped his memory.

Evidently the pygmy plans, whatever they might be, suffered a severe upset at the sight of the wall. The medley of consultation became louder. A tall figure came pushing through the crowd, and emerged from the main entrance. Mark recognised him for a European, and grinned at his expression of consternation. A quantity of animated explanation ensued, followed by a council of war.

Still Smith made no move. Mark wondered. A volley of sharp stones flung into the mob might have done considerable damage, although the range was long.

The pygmies came to a decision at last, and made the first of their mistakes. Possibly they believed that only a few men held the wall, but their tactics were crudely incautious. They consisted merely in stringing out to the full breadth of the cavern, and making a headlong charge. Smith let them cover fully half the distance before he gave a shout.

The defenders rose to their feet, and a volley of stones crashed into the foremost rank of runners. A number fell or stumbled. Those behind, unable to stop, pitched headlong over the fallen. Before they could rise a second volley descended on them—sharp-edged stones which seldom killed, but could cut and wound painfully. The line of attack was broken in several places by tangled heaps of dwarfs struggling to recover their feet, but the attack itself did not waver. The uninjured came charging on where the way was clear, with undiminished speed. The hail of stones was now continuous, but in spite of it many won through to the foot of the wall. There for the most part they stopped, dismayed, only a few attempted the futility of climbing. The rest stood at a loss, marks for the stone-throwers. Their only weapons were stone knives, and they bore no shields for protection. Their bewilderment was pathetic; the brave assault had become a tragic farce. Those who could, did the only possible thing; they turned and scuttled back the way they had come.

Ed's voice rang out in a Gargantuan bellow of laughter. This fight, after all their preparation, had turned out to be nothing but a huge joke. The whole army of the pygmies routed by a few showers of stones; the improvised clubs had not even been put to the test. Others joined in his laughter; it became a great, roaring gust sweeping backwards and forwards through the echoing cavern. Of the pygmies only a few lay still, the rest were limping alone or in mutually assisting couples back to the passage mouths whence the rolling rumble of laughter followed them.

Mark could not join in the laughter. It was too cruel, too contemptuous of the little men. He was as relieved as the rest to find that the fight was no fight, but he saw what the others seemed to miss. These pygmies, these sorrowful-eyed little men, were fighting to preserve their race. They knew, as well as he knew, that once the outside world should learn of their existence, the end would not be long in coming. They were primitives, as Gordon had said. Their only hope of continued existence was to remain segregated. Time and time again it had been shown that the primitive cannot co-exist with the modern. Not only is there decimation by disease, but there seems to grow within them a lethal discouragement. They cannot adapt. The capacity for mutation has been outgrown. They are fitted for no other world nor society but their own, and the unfit may not survive.

They had much of that complacency which primitive races frequently display, but their energy was not entirely sapped; they could still fight for existence, though they might not change. They had not admitted, or had not allowed themselves to admit, that their hopes were forlorn, their doom certain. If they could prevent the success of the tunnel, they must still contend with the water. They might block break after break as it occurred, but sooner or later it would get them. The New Sea would come pouring in through the airshafts to submerge their whole cave world as it had already flooded the lower levels. In the end they must be driven into the open, or trapped to drown down here.

Mark became unpleasantly reminded that he also was trapped. There were times when he could scarcely believe that the tunnel through the hundreds of feet of rock would ever be finished. It was an all but impossible task for men as ill equipped as they. Smith said 'any time now', but for how long—he asked himself again—had the prisoners been saying 'any time now'? And how could they tell? Who among them had any idea of their depth? The phrase was no more than an empty expression of hope; an article of faith to ward off apathy.

He found he had been gazing without sight upon one of the prone figures. It had not stirred; it never would stir. One side of its head had been broken in by a stone. Perhaps he had flung that stone.... He remembered Margaret's words:

'So horribly suddenly.... A minute ago they were running.... Oh, Mark, what have you done...?'

Why had he? He hadn't wanted to kill that little man. He'd never seen him before. He'd only wanted to stop him and his fellows—not to break them. That was how it always was—wasteful, senseless smashing of men.... His eyes wandered from the abandon of one sprawling form to the futility of another. There were ten altogether. Ed would think that funnier still—a battle with only ten casualties. Well, let him laugh. It was funny in a way: this human race which slaughtered members of itself. No one seemed to see it that way, even though they used a proverb about cutting one's nose to spite one's face. 'Queer lot we are,' he murmured to himself.

He shifted his gaze back to the passage-mouths. Most of the retreat had poured into the right-hand opening. He recalled that it was the one through which he had entered with Gordon; the link between this and the other fungus cave.

The defenders held to their posts, waiting for the next move. It was not likely that the pygmies would give up after one reverse. There was evidently a consultation in progress, for an occasional sound of high-pitched chatter floated in to them.

Smith decided that there was no immediate danger. The pygmy preparations might take some time. He detailed a party to relieve the tunnellers, and gave permission for the cord smokers to descend and continue their work. The rest sprawled at ease upon the wall top, some falling asleep, others talking. Ed sat down cross-legged and began to improve his mace by a further binding of cord which he had somehow acquired; he accompanied the task by a *sotte voce* cowboy song of startling obscenity. Gordon came wandering along the rampart, and sat down by Mark.

'Silly, isn't it?' he said, glancing at the bodies on the loam.

Mark nodded. 'Damn silly. I suppose it's the way we're made. Ten of the little chaps dead—and none of us a penny the worse or the better. Has Smith any idea of the next move?' he added.

'No,' Gordon shook his head. 'It's a case of wait and see.'

They chatted for some time in a desultory manner before Mark bethought him of the question he had meant to put.

'I can't get it out of my mind that I've seen people like these before. It's absurd, of course, because they can't have been photographed, but the type isn't altogether strange. What is it they're like?'

'Oh, you've noticed it, too, have you? They're pygmies.'

'No, I mean what race are they? I know they are pygmy sized.'

'They *are* pygmies—not a doubt of it. There's not only the size, but the shape of the head, odd proportions of their spindly limbs, and that curiously sad, solemn look characteristic of them. They're not so mournful really, it's a way pygmy faces have.'

Mark had a sudden memory of a travel film. Pygmies, diminutive against the exploring party, looking at the camera with large, bewildered eyes; every face, male or female, adult or child, stamped with the same die of permanent melancholy. That was it, of course; the half memory of that film had been lurking just out of reach. Queer that it had not occurred to him before: the selfsame expression—or was it lack of expression?—had stared from the faces of these troglodytes, but until Gordon had told him he could not place it. He had used the word 'pygmy' as he might have said 'dwarf', with no understanding of its significance. Yet it was not so odd that he should have missed the connection—these cave dwellers were a pale, dirty white.

'But pygmies are black,' he objected.

'The surface ones, but why should they be black down here? No sun; no need of pigmentation. These chaps were probably black enough when they came in. It'd work out through the generations. Look what one generation has done for the prisoners' children, the "natives", no sign of ruddy complexion there.'

'But hang it, there aren't any pygmies for hundreds of miles to the south of here.'

'Not now, but there were once—I've got a theory about these chaps and how they got here, if it's of any interest to you.'

Mark encouraged him to go on talking. If nothing more, it served to relieve the monotony of waiting for an attack which might never come.

'The most troublesome thing is,' Gordon began, 'that ever since I knew of their existence, I've not been able to verify any of my facts. If we do get out of this, I'm going to dig myself into the B.M. reading-room, and make certain either one way or the other. However, here's their history roughly, as I think it must be.

'You know that thousands of years ago the whole continent of Europe was far warmer than it is now? That has been proved in lots of ways from fossils and remains. Among other things, traces of elephants have been found near Cromer, where there was once a forest. Elephants, mind you, not mammoths. The mammoths didn't mind climates below zero, but the elephants have always required warmth. Furthermore, they have found the remains of the same species of elephant in Dorset, in a buried trench over twelve feet deep. Now nature doesn't dig trenches through layers of chalk and flint to catch elephants; but there's a creature that does, and that's man. That elephant died a hell of a long time ago because man was there to kill him.

'England was not yet an island. The present North Sea was a plain, connecting it with the continent. Subtropical fauna ranged and thrived there, but even then there were our ancestors to harry it into traps and slay it by other cunning. It is a common fault to put the appearance of man at too late a date. After all, we had to evolve, like the other species. There is still a tendency (it may be a lingering respect for Genesis) to picture man appearing suddenly and fully formed, to the great consternation of all the other denizens of the world. He did not. He climbed as slowly and painfully as the rest. Perhaps those men who hunted elephants across North Europe did not look much like us, but even at that remote date, they were a long jump ahead of the animals they slew.

'Nor were the men all of one type. They, like the other creatures, had adapted to different climates. Until they had evolved clothes, discovered fire and other means of protection from extreme heat and cold, they were as subject to natural conditions as the animals themselves. Each race must have lived in its own zone with very little trespassing either to north or south.

'But in the course of time, the zones shifted. The earth's axis tilted; the sub-tropical flora began to perish. Each summer there was a little more ice round the poles, and each winter saw the Arctic Circle pushed a little farther south. It was slow—a matter of a few inches at a time—but it was relentless. The ice crept down, driving everything before it. The winters grew harder and longer; the animals went south, and the hunters followed. North Europe became temperate, then cold. Still the ice pursued, and the men from the north were driven down upon the inhabitants of the torrid lands in the south.

'The races did not mix. The original inhabitants were

a smaller, weaker species than the invaders, and unable to resist the successive waves of humanity rolling in from the north; they were, in fact, the ancestors of the pygmies. The northerners were a hardier, more adaptable race for whom life had been less easy than it was for the others; there could be no question which was the better fitted to survive. There was a natural limit to the number which the land could support, and it became clear that if anyone was going to perish through starvation, it would not be the newcomers. The pygmies took their chance of survival and began to migrate southward in their turn. They took to the great forests, and hid themselves in jungle depths so inhospitable and unattractive that no race has ever yet troubled to dislodge them.

'It was one of the great changes of the world. The ice caps, creeping closer from north and south, compressed all life into the equatorial belt. Not only were the pygmies driven south, but other, similar races in other parts of the world were forced from the open, fertile country to seek refuges where they might survive. About that time the Andamanese must have reached their islands, the Sakai have found Sumatra, the Semangs, Borneo, and the New Guinea Pygmies have hidden themselves in their impenetrable country. And there they have all remained, for though the ice receded, the invaders did not. Their progeny spread to cover the north once again, but there was no racial withdrawal from the southern lands. That is what I meant when I said that these were real pygmies.'

'That this was once all pygmy country, and these have survived?'

'Exactly. They were driven into inhospitable regions; they took to living in caves. They found that this district was riddled with them, and they went deeper. Though, mind you, none of this happened suddenly; it was an instinctive move for self-preservation going on for generation after generation as conditions grew worse; there can have been little of conscious flight about it. While some made for the jungles they have never left, others reverted to cave dwelling, withdrawing more and more, spending less and less of their time on the surface, hiding from a world in which they could not compete, until at last there came generations who knew the outside only from hearsay as a place of discouragement and terror. So the elders died and the last link was snapped; communication with the surface ceased. They dug themselves deep into the earth. They joined cavern with cavern to form a subterranean country. They learned how to grow the giant fungi for food, and retained the secret of manufacturing their luminous fluid. In the end the life of the outer world became no more than a tradition kept alive by the occasional arrival of wanderers such as ourselves. The dominant races pursued their appointed course on the surface: the memory of the pygmies grew fainter until, at last, it was entirely rubbed away, and they were forgotten, lost.'

There was silence for a time after Gordon stopped speaking. Mark considered the theory. Fantastic, of course, but then, so was the pygmies' presence, and there must be some explanation of it. There could be no doubt that the caverns had been inhabited for a very long time. The fact that no tradition survived above indicated an immense period of utter isolation.

'When do you think all this happened?' he asked.

Gordon shrugged his shoulders. 'Hard to say. Somewhere in the Lower Paleolithic, I should guess—towards the end of it, about the Acheulean.'

'No,' said Mark. 'Tell me in English. How many years?'

Gordon considered for a moment. 'Perhaps a hundred thousand years.'

'A—what?' Mark blinked.

'Yes, I mean it. The trouble with people like you is that you have such a poor idea of the antiquity of man. I tell you that the pygmies represent one of the oldest living races, and you're staggered by a hundred thousand years. It's a mere flea-bite in natural development. Why, Piltdown man probably lived three times as long ago as that. The effect of all this Genesis business is to make people believe that nothing ever happened before about 2000 B.C. assure you it did, and it had been happening for a long time.

'Just to cheer you up, I'll admit that there are two bad snags I've struck. One is those Egyptian gods, and the other is these lights.' He glanced up at the roof. 'They've really got me beat—in spite of what I said before—and the containers are more puzzling than the fluid inside them. I don't see how these people, virtually a stone-age race, found out how to make 'em—nor what they're made of, for that matter. In fact, they're the weakest spot in the whole theory, blast them. If it wasn't for the lights, they could never have——'

He stopped suddenly. Mark, looking up, saw that a few white figures had reappeared in the passage mouths. A shout from Smith called everyone to the top of the barrier. A score or so of pygmies emerged, and strung out into a line close to the back wall. Each was carrying something which it was impossible to determine at their distance.

Since there was no longer anything to be gained by surprise, the defenders had no reason to lie low. A volley of stones hurtled towards the dwarfs. The majority fell short, and those, which did not, were so spent that they could easily be dodged.

'No good,' grumbled the man beyond Gordon. 'Better wait till they come on a bit.'

But the pygmies were in no hurry. Each was doing something with the instrument he carried.

'What's their little game?' added the speaker.

A moment later he knew. The pygmies swung their right arms, and a flight of sharp stones whistled through the air. One took him full in the face, toppling him backwards off the wall. Mark, Gordon, and the rest dropped hurriedly to full length behind the parapet.

'Slings. Damn it, why didn't we think of them?' Gordon muttered.

Mark put his eye to his former spyhole. The slings were putting up a barrage which whistled low over his head. Something issuing from the right-hand tunnel caused him to give a whistle of surprise. Gordon risked his head above the edge to see what had caused it; he kept it there until a stone thudded against a trunk unpleasantly close.

'Ingenious devils,' he said, ducking again.

The round head of a mushroom, looking like a huge, unpainted archery target, slowly emerged into their caves. Once in the open, it moved sideways to make room for another following behind it, and slightly forward to allow the slingers to throw over it from their back wall position. The second mushroom head drew out and ranged itself alongside the first. Another followed, and another until a long rank was formed.

The fungi had been felled with particular care not to sever the heads. The trunk was carried by several men, while the round top made an excellent shield for them. When the first rank of portable defences was complete, a second was begun. Not until three such lines had been formed did the advance start. Then they moved forward slowly and deliberately, keeping their formation while the slingmen, acting as artillery, kept up a ceaseless shower of sharp stones.

'They've got the right idea,' said Gordon, with detached admiration. 'Pygmy tanks now in action.'

The opposition to the advance was slight as yet, being confined to a few experimental stones pitched uselessly against the mushroom heads. As the front rank passed the half-way stage, Ed rose to his feet and hurled a stone with all his force. It struck one of the white circles with an audible thud, and embedded itself in the pulpy mass. There was no other result. Ed dropped back with a grunt of disgust. Several others risked the slingmen, and imitated him with as little success; those stones which did not bounce off stayed to stud the white circles with dark flecks. The advance never hesitated.

Smith sent word down the line for clubs to be got ready. It looked like hand-to-hand fighting, for the pygmies would be able to advance under cover to the foot of the wall. So far the defenders had no apprehension of real trouble; their attitude was still an appreciation of the little men's ingenuity. After all, what could the attackers do? Merely attempt to scale the wall; it would be easy enough to push them off.

The advancing ranks increased the angle of the mushroom heads until, when they reached the wall, they were upright, forming a roof upon which missiles rained down. Only three had failed to make the journey, having stopped when their carriers were struck by lucky rather than skilful shots.

Against the wall they stopped. The defenders were unable to see what was taking place, but it was guessed that the facing of mushroom heads was either having footholds cut in it, or being pulled down to expose the more easily climbable trunk ends. A sudden diversion occurred. Mark heard one of their men shout, and saw him pointing to the passages. More figures were entering. They were pallid, like the rest, but taller, and better built.

'Good Lord, they've got the "natives" with 'em,' Gordon murmured.

The slingmen were still in action, so that the 'natives' covered the first few yards at a crouching run, keeping their heads below the line of fire. As they drew nearer they straightened up and increased their pace. An intensified fire from the slingers still kept the defenders behind their parapet. The leading 'natives' rushed across the ground, and climbed upon the rear rank of mushroom heads. It became clear that the pygmies' intentions had been not only to provide shields for themselves, but to make a platform upon which the 'natives' could be brought more nearly to the height of the defenders.

The slingers stopped as the 'natives' climbed and ran on. The defenders rose, hurling a shower of stones. The 'natives' were in great majority, but at severe disadvantage. It was difficult to move fast over the uneven platform, and they were fully exposed at short range. Their only arms were stone knives. Nevertheless, they came on. Before long they were battling with the men at the wall. Mark's stone club rose and fell with the rest. He struck without anger, coolly and shrewdly. He did not seem able to develop a fighting rage against these men. He aimed at the shoulders, content to numb the arms; he had still a feeling that this was a kind of mock battle, part of a great misunderstanding.

They were fighting now all along the line, and most of the men were not using his half-hearted tactics. They fought to kill or maim. Mark supposed that his freshness made the difference; had he been here for years like many of them, he would have known how they felt. Along in the middle of the line he could see Smith hammering away with a short club in each hand, while Ed made flailing sweeps with his mace.

The momentary lull passed as a fresh rush of 'natives' came on. One dodged within Mark's guard, tearing a ragged scrape on his upper arm. It was nothing much; he scarcely felt it, but it served to change his outlook. He began to lay about him in real earnest. Another man caught hold of his club, and tried to wrench it away. Mark's left fist came up with all his strength to the right of the other's jaw. The man reeled away, and the next comer felt the full weight of the club. The fury of the attack began to slacken; the 'natives' were losing heart or growing less rash. Mark lowered his arm and stood panting, only to square up swiftly as another white figure came charging at him. He swung up his club, but at the same moment the support beneath his left foot fell away, and he tripped. His club was knocked from his hand, and the 'native' bounded over the parapet almost upon him. He fended off a vicious swipe of the stone knife, and caught the man's right wrist. For some seconds the two rolled this way and that in attempts to get the upper hand, then the 'native' suddenly went limp. Mark looked up to see Gordon bending over them.

'Thanks!' he said.

He was lying in a shallow depression between two of the white trunks. A depression which he was quite certain had not been there a few minutes ago. One trunk must suddenly have subsided, and in doing so, upset him. But why?

He crawled to a spot where he could look over the back of the wall, and found himself gazing into a pygmy face. Without hesitation he crashed a fist into it, and sent the owner tumbling backwards. There were others down there. But how had they got past the wall? He looked along and saw one in the act of emerging from a hole. The pygmies must have withdrawn logs from several places in the wall, under cover of their platform. In some spots those above were so jammed as to leave a way right through, whereas in others, such as that directly below him, the logs above had fallen down to close the hole. He caught up his fallen club, and sprang down with a shout. Only about a dozen of the pygmies were through so far, and when four or five other men joined him, they were soon accounted for. It became necessary, however, to set a guard on the holes to prevent more getting through.

'Just as well I fell when I did,' Mark thought. 'A few more minutes, and they'd have been in in dozens.'

He stood watching a hole in the middle of the wall. He was glad of the rest, for he had nothing to do now but keep an eye on it, and bring down his club on anything that came out of it.

'Hey?' called a voice above him.

He looked up to see Ed's tousled, full-bearded head.

'Get me one of those puff-balls, will you? A ripe one, buddy, and handle with care.'

'What about this?' Mark pointed to the hole.

'That's O.K. I'll watch it.'

Mark obediently sought one of the largest puff-balls and trundled it gingerly up to the wall.

'Can you lift it?' Ed inquired.

Mark could, with some difficulty, for it was a cumbersome object. Ed reached down as far as possible, and between them they managed to get it intact to the top of the wall. There Ed sat down and began carefully to cut long incisions with a sharp stone. Mark stood below with attention divided between Ed's operations, and his guardianship of the hole. He was puzzled, for there was fighting still going on along the wall, and it was unlike Ed not to be in the thick of it.

'What's it for?' he asked.

Ed chuckled. 'Come up and see.'

Mark climbed back to the wall top and sat down. A head was at once thrust experimentally out of the hole below. Mark dropped a stone on it, and it was withdrawn.

Ed continued to make incisions radiating like meridians from the poles of the puff-ball. None of the cuts was deep enough to split the skin, but the whole was weakened almost to bursting-point. The fighting had now become half-hearted, compared with the first attack. Probably its object had been to keep the defenders employed while the pygmies climbed through their holes in the wall. Now that the rear attack had not come, the 'natives' were flagging.

Ed examined his puff-ball, and grinned with satisfaction. He picked it up, raising it with both hands above his head. For a moment he poised, then he swayed forward, heaving with all his weight. The ball lobbed into the crowd of attackers. Two 'natives' went down beneath it as it burst. A cloud of white spores broke out like a flurry of snow. The men close to it were blotted from sight. A sound of coughing and spluttering arose from within the drifting mist. As it spread, growing more tenuous, the figures of 'natives' became visible, bent double in paroxysms of coughing, while with each breath they took, they drew more of the irritating feathery spores into their lungs. The cloud of white dust spread wider, afflicting more of the attackers. They lost all capability of fighting. Their eyes streamed so that they could barely see; they staggered to and fro, sneeezing, gasping, wheezing like the worst asthmatics. Ed gave a bellow of delighted laughter.

'Hey, gimme your jacket, and fetch another,' he directed.

He began to swing the coat before him, fanning the drifting spores away from the wall.

Within a few minutes there was a haze of spores all along the line, and the defenders had abandoned their clubs in favour of ragged improvised fans. The 'natives' were hopelessly demoralised. They could do little more than stagger, so exhausted were they with their efforts to cough up the fungus dust. The pygmies, below their testudo of mushroom heads, were in little better plight, for they had begun to breathe the spores which filtered through from above. Those who were not deafened by the sound of their own and other's coughing must have ground their teeth with anger as the familiar roar of laughter rose once more from the defenders. There was nothing to be done. They were too hopelessly disorganised for further action. As best they could they crawled free of their mushroom shields and made their way, an orderless, anomalous crowd of choking, sneezing miserables, back to the passage mouths. Gusts of laughter from the wall harried them on.

Ed, in a state of uproarious childish delight at the success of his 'gas attack', flung jibes after the rout. Zickle had broken into some heathen chant of victory. Even Mark found himself laughing at the farcical climax of this second attack.

The last gasping pygmy fled from the sound of jubilation, but the hilarity continued. It took Smith a long time to impress on his followers that it was necessary to repair their defences.

CHAPTER VII

MARK looked up at Smith.

'It must be several days since that second attack. Do you really think they'll come on again?'

'Sure thing,' Smith nodded emphatically. 'Why else'd I have gotten the wall mended?' He looked across at Gordon, who agreed.

'They're sure to try to get us one way or another. They can't afford to let us escape at any cost in casualties.'

'But it's so long since that puff-ball business. They may have given up.'

'Not they. I reckon they're putting their heads together and thinking up a new dodge.' Smith paused. 'What gets me is the ingenuity of 'em last time,' he continued. 'Another few minutes and there'd have been hundreds of 'em through the wall. Didn't guess the little guys had it in them to think up a stunt like that.'

'They haven't,' said Gordon. 'I'll bet anything you like that Miguel or one of his crowd put them up to it; what's more, its ten to one that whoever did it is putting them up to another one now. Don't forget, this means a lot to them—just as much as it does to us. They are out to nail us, and as a matter of fact, if they do give Miguel the run of the outer caves, he stands a better chance of getting out than we do.'

'Well, in that case,' said Mark thoughtfully, 'what are we here for?'

The others stared at him.

'I mean if we surrender and Miguel gets out, he won't keep quiet about this place. There'll be an expedition down here—just as there will be if we get out—so if he's got a better chance, why not let him go willingly?'

'You're forgetting something.'

'I don't see——'

'You're forgetting that Miguel made a bargain with the pygmies. I don't know what pygmy morals on a point like that are, but why should they keep it? He's got no way of making them keep it that I can see. Suppose they're just using him? They must know what his little game is, sure enough, but they won't let him play it.'

'Besides,' Gordon broke in, 'if they can beat a hundred and fifty of us, they'll ask themselves why they should kowtow to Miguel and his lot—and they'll find there's no reason why they should. The thing I don't understand is his falling for their promises. It's not like his kind to do a deal without guarantees.'

The three were silent for a time. It was Mark again who spoke first.

'I should have thought,' he said, 'that it would have been a good move from their point of view to put those lights out.' He looked up at the blue-white globes, shimmering unharmed in the rocky roof. 'The confusion would just about put paid to our defence: they'd be almost certain to break through somewhere.'

'Several reasons,' Gordon explained. 'For one thing they're not easy to break. They may look like glass, but they're tough. And, for another, these pygmies are more scared of the dark than any kid. It's just about the worst kind of bogey to them. Maybe you didn't realise it, but they've spent all their lives under these lamps, and that's tied up with the third reason. It'd be sacrilege to bust them. Their lives depend on them, and they all but worship them.' At Mark's look of inquiry he amplified: 'They're symbols of Ra—you remember, he was holding one in that carving. If they break one, they are insulting him. If they break several, he is so angry that he sends darkness to plague them. According to Mahmud they are so used to light that they can't think of darkness as being just an absence of it, but they fear it as a concrete something by which Ra manifests displeasure. It's for that reason more than any other that they're so scared of it. And even that's not a new idea—I seem to remember something about a plague of darkness over Egypt, and the Egyptians didn't like that, much though they knew what night meant. For these little devils it must be terrifying—like being struck blind.'

Mark was scarcely convinced. Destruction of the lights seemed such an obvious way to create utter confusion. The globes might be tough, but the pygmies' slung stones travelled forcefully.... They were not unbreakable; he remembered Gordon's own story of one smashed experimentally. Such a superstition as Gordon suggested seemed a slender screen between themselves and chaos. He said as much. Gordon shook his head.

'It's the safest defence we could have. There's no better guarantee than a good, well-grounded superstition. The decisions of the Hague Court or a Geneva conference are flimsy compared with it. You read a bit of anthropology one day—it'll surprise you. People can bind fetters round themselves that they can never break—though they may be beyond reason and safety.' His voice grew quieter and less emphatic as he ruminated: 'Superstition and suggestion through superstition are greatly neglected powers nowadays. I don't mean that there aren't plenty of superstitious conventions and taboos about; there are, but they're formless and ill-controlled, and very often conflicting. There's a great influence over men and women just wasted and running to seed today. Instead of using it, the leaders have dropped it. The only way they attempt to control people now is by mass suggestion at a late age. That works, but it's inefficient; it has to be boosted continually. You can easily work up a nation to war pitch, but it takes continuous energetic propaganda to keep it there. If you allow them to think for themselves, they'll slack off, and it becomes progressively more difficult to keep up your propaganda so that they shan't think for themselves sooner or later. What's more, mass suggestion always begets a certain amount of counter mass suggestion—pure cussedness to begin with, as likely as not, but it goes on growing because of the defaulters who join it when they find they've been hoaxed by the original suggestion. Damned silly way of going on. Reminds me of those advertisements about increasing your height—it can be done, but the right time to do it is while you're young. In the same way, suggestion will work on an adult, but if you want to make a good job of it you've got to start on the infant. The church has the right idea. It got in as soon as it decently could with a baptism service. When they followed that up with a proper course of training, they'd got the poor little blighter just where they wanted him. He couldn't think for himself. He thought he could, mind you; he often thought he was doing no end of a fine think, but that didn't matter; he was only playing a kind of game with the rules already set in his mind. In practice, he was only crawling around in a mental pen.

'That was the way with most of the old religions, and a lot of them lasted a long time. They bust up mostly because they used their power wrongly, not because it weakened. Some of them didn't give enough crawling room; they drew the walls of the pen closer and closer until something was bound to give. Others let the walls fall into disrepair so that the people inside could look out and see that the country round about wasn't so bad after all. And then they lost their great power—all the western nations have lost it, but a good superstitious upbringing still holds the primitives.'

'That was a sign that the power of superstition was ending,' Mark interrupted. 'The people were turning to reason instead.'

'Reason, my foot. They won't be ready for reason for thousands of years—if they last that long. My God, just look at the world, man. Reason!'

'But it's true. The religions are dying—in the west, anyhow. I know people make a vulgar noise about them, but that's because they're not convinced—if they were, there'd be no reason for the noise.'

'Rot. The religions aren't dying. Just because you give a thing a different name it doesn't change it. You can have a religion without an anthropomorphic figure-head, just as you can have a state without a king. Democracy, Socialism, Communism, they're all religions.'

Mark objected. 'No, they're political theories.'

'Well, when did you ever find a religion that wasn't somehow bound up with a political theory? I tell you they are just as much religions as Christianity, Mohammedanism, or Buddhism. They are a superstition. What else but a superstition could produce the fantastic idea that all men are equal? Reason certainly could not. What but superstition could set people forming laws on a Lowest Common Denominator basis, and forcing brilliant intellects to abide by them? Is it a home of reason which devotes so much of its energy and wealth to preserving its unfit that its fit are neglected and become unfit themselves? And these, mind you, are recent developments among people whom you say are "turning to reason". Reason! Oh, my God!'

Gordon got up and stumped away. Smith grinned at Mark.

'Great guy on the spielin', ain't he? Only trouble is that he doesn't know what he wants any more than the rest of us. Still, it's been handy havin' him around; gets the boys talkin' and arguin' so that they forget 'emselves for a bit.' He got up. 'I'm goin' over to have a look at Ed and his bunch. Comin'?'

They made a detour and came upon the group from the rear. Certain parts of the cave had become unhealthy since Ed's artillery school had started. Slings are instruments requiring a nicety of operation only to be attained by practice, wherefore the danger area in front of the tyros was of considerable width. In a mushroom head, leaned against the wall for target duty, two stones had lodged. Ed turned his usual cheerful countenance.

'Made it—once,' he declared proudly.

'Out of how many?' Smith asked.

'Oh, lay off that. This ain't a Tommy gun—you gotta get to know it.'

'Whose is the other?'

'Zickle's. That nigger's gonna do big things.'

Zickle gave a show of white teeth.

'Yes, me gottim,' he agreed.

The two stood watching the practice for a while. The speed and force of the missiles was formidable, though the aim remained erratic. Ed, undiscouraged, pointed out that when the attack should come there would be a lot of targets, not just one.

As they wandered on, leaving him to it, Mark inquired as to progress on the tunnel. Smith answered him with the usual 'any time now'.

'Do you know what's above?' Mark jerked his thumb at the roof.

'Not for sure. What're you gettin' at?'

'Just this—suppose it's a hill or a mountain?'

'Well?'

'Well, you may have got up beyond normal surface-level already, and be boring your way through the heart of a mountain.'

'It's possible—but it ain't likely. You see, there's a hell of a lot more flat than mountains round here. It's thousands to one against our being under any sizeable mountain, and I guess we've got to take the risk anyway.'

'You couldn't send out some side tunnels experimentally?'

Smith shook his head.

'Not now. It'd be a waste of time. If it hadn't come to a showdown, it might've been worth trying. But with this on our hands, the best we can do is to keep straight on and up.'

The two strolled on, talking until they were interrupted by a hail from the wall. Smith hurried over.

'What is it?'

'Something going on in the right-hand tunnel,' said the lookout. 'There've been one or two of them dodging about in there.'

Both Smith and Mark stared, but they could make out little. There was certainly movement, though it was impossible to make out what was taking place.

'Better call the men up,' Smith decided. 'There may be another charge.'

Within two minutes the parapet was lined with staring faces whose owners speculated audibly, but it was half an hour before a definite move took place.

Near the middle of the wall Ed had chosen to station himself and his 'artillery'. The rest gave them a wide berth, and eyed them with misgiving; it had been noticed that stones had a habit of flying out of slings before the release was intended.

At last, when the majority had decided that the alarm must be false, a few small, white figures issued from the right-hand cave mouth. Ed waited until they had formed a line, then he and his men let fly. Most of the stones clattered harmlessly; only one figure subsided. It sat on the ground, hugging a damaged knee. The rest swung their slings and replied with a volley. The men on the wall watched the missiles come arching towards them. They were bigger than the stones used before, and flung on a higher trajectory. They looked like a flight of snowballs. Only when they landed did it become clear that they were not stones at all.

One struck the parapet just in front of Mark. It burst into a cloud of spores. He began to cough and choke as they entered his lungs. The more he gasped for breath, the more floating spores he breathed. His eyes streamed until he could scarcely see. He had a glimpse of another volley of white balls, bursting in another smother of spores.

The whole line of men was gasping and choking in the dusty air. The flakes swirled around them like a mist, blotting everything from view. Throats and chests began to ache with coughing; each fresh paroxysm seemed to rack more painfully.

They had been out-manoeuvred. The pygmies, or their advisers, had welcomed Ed's fungus idea, but they had realised too that they could not hope in the face of a bombardment to roll the puff-balls up to the wall. The problem had been solved by extracting the spores from ripe balls, and stitching them into smaller skins suitable for slinging. But to what purpose?

The wall with its defenders had now disappeared into an artificial blizzard, but the flights of spore-bombs continued to fall with accuracy wherever the cloud was thinning. The pygmies and 'natives' could not hope to make an attack now. Once they should reach the spore area they would be in as bad a plight as the rest. It could only be that the present barrage was intended not just to disable, but to act as a screen. What might be afoot at the end of the cave, the spluttering, choking defenders could only guess.

At last, after what seemed an interminable period, the spore-bombs ceased to fall. The white swirl began to settle and thin, or drift away. The paroxysms of choking grew less frequent and less agonising. Eyelids could be opened without reclosing immediately in self-defence. The red-rimmed eyes, still streaming, could peer painfully in an effort to see what had taken place behind the screen, but their vision was dimly blurred. It was noses which gave the clue—a faint smell of burning.

A whistling flight of stones made them duck again. Mark put his recovering eyes to the spyhole, and the pygmy operations ceased to be a mystery.

In a line across the end of the cave lay five huge piles of

vegetable rubbish, and from each was ascending a column of heavy, yellow smoke. For a few feet it poured straight up, then it bent over, broadening fanwise as the draught from the tunnels behind began to carry it farther into the big cavern. The rising curls, progressively attenuated, mingled as they climbed, losing individuality in a grey-yellow haze. Already an obscuring tide was flowing across the uneven roof. Those lamps it had engulfed showed wanly; their brilliance sicklied to a gloomy dimness. Mark watched it lap about others, flowing first to either side before it thickened to submerge them; increasing the gloom step by step.

With the decreasing light, the cave seemed to change character. It was no longer the familiar, workaday place they all knew. Nooks and corners, becoming shrouded, took on an ill aspect. Fears were born in the hidden crevices and came stealing out to attack the men's minds; the *agents provocateurs* of panic.

A group on the far right swarmed over the parapet and dropped to the loam. They started racing for the fires, oblivious of the flying stones which slashed at them. The slingmen changed their tactics and sent spore bombs which burst in their path. The running men staggered and reeled, they doubled up, and the sound of their rasping coughs came back to those still on the wall. The stones whistled among them again, felling a number and driving the rest into an impotent fury as they floundered with a temporary blindness.

Mark glanced round at Smith in mute inquiry. The other shook his head.

'No good. That's just what they want—to get us in the open. Once they do that it's all up.'

Smith was right; it was the position, not the numbers of the defenders which had baffled the attack. Doubtless they would be able to give a good account of themselves with their clubs, but though the pygmies were small, their numbers, added to those of the 'natives', were not. To take to the open meant certain defeat sooner or later. Mark became gloomy. This smoke business had not been foreseen. The slight draught which played through the crevices would not be enough to keep the air breathable. The time would not be long in coming when the only alternatives would be to make a dash or to suffer asphyxiation. Either meant the end of their plan. The pygmies would probably prefer the latter; it would give them less trouble.

The smoke was now a thick blanket over the whole roof. In the semi-darkness the men looked questioningly at their leader. Smith failed them—he could see no way out, and their eyes, roving farther along the wall, sought the burly Ed. He, too, was without a suggestion, and for the first time in Mark's experience of him, looked dejected.

'No, you ain't got this thing right,' he said to those who urged a charge. 'Maybe you'll get five minutes' fun skull cracking, but that ain't gonna help us any if you get your own skulls cracked after. What we gotta do is figure out some new line. And,' he added after an interval, 'it seems to me as there ain't none.... Gees, don't I wish I'd never pulled that puff-ball stuff.'

The smoky stratum deepened; the cave grew more fearful in murky penumbra. The yellow columns above the five fires intensified, appearing almost as writhing solids. It was a mere matter of time till the pall above should creep down to drive them from the wall. Beyond the fires, to windward of the choking smoke, the slingers stood waiting; behind them, others filled the passages impassably. Sheer clogging of numbers alone would defeat an attempt to rush.

The defenders, too, waited. They could do nothing else. The fate of the first party to go over the top had proved a potent lesson. They could no longer look to Smith or any other as leader. That fatalism which they had thrown off at the need for action came seeping back, tinged now with resentful desperation. The tunnel upon which so many of them had worked for years would never be used now. The phrase, 'any time now' had even less meaning than before. The last ray of their hope was narrowed by a closing iris of smoke until it became that ultimate pinpoint of light without which they could not live. It was that last, feeble glimmer which set one and then another pair of eyes roving towards the shadowed wall in unadmitted faith that a figure might yet emerge crying: 'We're through.' But no such figure showed. The wall and the tunnel they had hewn through it receded into a blacker and blacker distance....

'If only there were something we could *do,*' Gordon was muttering. 'To be smoked out like a lot of rats....'

There came a sudden noise, reverberating, booming in the shadows behind them. A hundred pairs of eyes switched like one towards it, boring the impenetrable. A sudden cry from the Negro, Zickle—'Water!' Then other voices, on rising, panicky notes—'Water! ... Water! ...'

Long minutes of chaos, kaleidoscopic. Shouts. Men gasping, cursing, dropping from the wall. Beyond, shrill pygmy voices rising in alarm. A last, disregarded volley from the slingers. Screams from the passage mouths. Fighting to escape, trampling one another, jammed in the tunnels? A hand on Mark's arm, rigid as a clamp. Gordon's voice, calm and firm among the hubbub. What's he saying?

'Wait. You'll be trampled.'

Wait! With the water gushing in to drown them all?

A wrench which failed to shake the clamp loose. Smith's voice:

'Plenty of time—plenty of time. Wait.'

First panic ebbing. Fighting for control. Behind it all, the rush of the water. Tons of it, spewing into the cave, reaching out to swamp and choke. Partial victory. It's a big cave—take a lot of water to fill it. Screams and shouts from the passages. Fighting, tearing one another to bits like animals—mad with fright. Gordon talking calmly to Smith:

'Let 'em get clear; the tunnel's narrow, it can't pass much water. Plenty of time.'

What tunnel? Things began to get clearer. Their tunnel, of course. It was through. Must have come up under the New Sea. Never thought of that possibility. The tunnel which was to lead to freedom.... Mark began to laugh with an odd giggle.

Gordon shook him violently.

'Stop it.'

Mark tried, but could not. It was irresistibly funny—the tunnel which was to lead to freedom....

Something hard and angular hit his jaw.

'Shut up—do you hear?'

The shaking went on. He stopped laughing. Queer, it hadn't been very funny after all. The shaking ceased.

'Sorry,' he said. Smith grunted, rubbing his knuckles.

Ed came ambling along the wall with several others trailing after him.

'Crazy bunch o' saps,' he observed, nodding in the direction of the passages. 'Can you beat it?' He spat disgustedly over the parapet. They listened for a moment to the sounds of strife mingling with the rush of the water.

'Gees, and I thought some of those guys got brains—if they have, they're on vacation right now.'

'Some of 'em'll get out,' said Smith.

'Sure they'll get out—an' for what? To be chased by the water. You know darned well there ain't no way for it to get outa this place. They'll go right up to the big first cave by the entrance—and then what? Jest wait right there until the water ups and catches 'em. Ain't that a hell of a fine way to die?'

They turned and looked over the ground behind the wall. The water was visible now; its edge had advanced to within a few feet of them and was crawling rapidly forward, stirring the loam to mud.

'Well, it'll soon put out those goddam fires,' Ed murmured philosophically.

'Look there.' Gordon pointed to the white circle of a puff-ball, just visible in the gloom. It was swaying and bobbing erratically on the flood.

'Well, what about it?'

'It's floating. These trunks will float, too. A couple of them lashed together would make a good raft for three or four men.'

'But we'd only go up there.' Mark looked up at the smoke curtain over the roof.

'No. We can float them out through the passages as the water rises. Float them right out to the first cave, and then——'

He stopped suddenly as Ed's huge hand smote him on the back.

'Atta boy! You've said it. Gimme some cord, somebody; I'm gonna get busy.'

The binding of several stone clubs was speedily untwisted. Within a few minutes all the men were lashing the thick, white trunks into pairs. The water rose and trickled through the wall as they worked. The five fires went out in bursts of steam and fierce sizzlings. The first completed raft was thrust over the parapet, and fell with a splash. Its two builders climbed after it. Another splash followed, and another, until all the rafts bobbed in the muddy water. Ed looked up at the last pair.

'C'm on, you guys. Time to go places. Snap into it.'

They swarmed down into knee-deep water, and waded forward, pushing their rafts towards the passages. Behind them still sounded the roar of gushing water; around the walls it lapped slowly higher....

PART III

CHAPTER I

MARGARET woke, and her first sight was a rock roof. It was seven feet above her, but it seemed to press down. Those tons of stone could be suspended safely, she hoped, above her body, but there was no support to lift them clear of her spirit. All that weight rested full upon it, striving to crush her stubborn resistance. This was always the worst moment of her 'day'. All defences were at their weakest, reserves at their ebb. She liked to keep her eyes closed when she woke, gathering strength before opening them.

How many times had she lain awake, but voluntarily blind, hoping futilely that it was a dream? She did not know. At first she had tried to keep some count of time, but she had missed once—or was it twice? She made two strokes on the wall, and then changed her mind and rubbed one out. Later she missed again. The record became a muddle. Anyhow, what was the good of it? Even if her sleeping periods did roughly correspond to nights in the world above, there was little to be gained from knowing how days, weeks, months slipped away. It did not help. Indeed, it made things worse. Without dates one could imagine the world as one had last seen it. Dates meant change outside, and it was somehow bitter to think of a world which went on changing, of seasons coming and going, flowers blooming and dying while one lay here inmured, dead to it all.

Yes, dead to it—only death must be more peaceful. Why did she not kill herself? On every waking she asked the same question. Sometimes she had resolved to do it, but then, with the fuller return of consciousness, she had absolved herself. Time for that later, after all, there were still possibilities.... When she had grown older, when her skin had lost its softness, and her hair become grey—when, in fact, there would be nothing to return to in the outside world; then she would do it.

She put up a hand and dragged a lock of hair forward over her face. Holding it out at full length, she could, by squinting uncomfortably, focus upon it. Presently she smoothed it back into place. Careful inspection had failed to reveal a single strand of grey among the dark red. There were stories of people whose hair had gone grey in a night—in view of the condition of her own, she was inclined to consider them fables; if they were not, she ought, she felt, to be snow-white by this time. Perhaps at the sides...?

An awkward business, this, and not a mirror to be had.

She sat up. A bundle of muddy-yellow fur in another corner uncurled, yawned widely and stretched itself. It sat back on its haunches, blinking at her.

'Good morning, Bast.'

The cat yawned again and, dropping its eyes, began the morning toilet.

'Yes,' she agreed. 'Bath time.'

She rose from the heap of fungus strips which did duty for a bed, and walked towards the entrance. It was necessary to stoop as she passed into the corridor; the place had been hewn by pygmies for the use of pygmies.

Outside, she greeted her guards. Her first resentment of them had long since passed off. What was the use? They no longer worried her; she had even begun to feel half sorry for them. At bottom they were nothing but simple, unmalicious little folk who had been cheated of life.

The usual procession formed up. First, two white dwarfs whose only garment was strictly utilitarian, consisting of a string about the waist for the purpose of supporting a stone knife. Then herself in that white suit which had been so smart, and was now so much the worse for wear. Finally, two more pygmies carrying slings and a pouch each of stones to supplement their knives. In this formation the five marched to the half-flooded cave which did duty as a swimming bath.

An air of ceremony had gathered about Margaret's ablutions. The operation designed purely for practical ends had succeeded in becoming a popular spectacle. Numbers of impressed spectators, apparently with nothing to do, attended it as in other circumstances they might have attended the changing of the guard.

She seldom thought without a smile of the agitation

which had accompanied her first swim. She had been in the water before her guards had realised her intention. The terrible howl of lamentation which greeted her reappearance on the surface could not be attributed entirely to disinterested anxiety for her safety. What penalties were visited on guards who allowed a semi-sacred person to elude them either by suicide or escape, she never inquired, but probably they were painful. She had turned her head to look up at them, whereat the howls had languished, to be replaced by expressions of wonder. An excited gabble arose as she struck out, and when she swam back to the ledge, it was to land at the feet of a group astonished into awe and servility.

At that time she had been unable either to speak or to understand their language, but it needed no words to show that she had risen in their estimation. Her divinity, first suspected owing to her association with Bast, was now an established fact. She felt the difference in their regard, and resolved that the advantage should not be allowed to lapse. She pursued it by making her 'daily' swim a custom.

On this 'morning'—the habit of dividing her time into manageable sections persisted in the face of their inaccuracy—the ceremony was performed as usual. A crowd of a hundred or so persons who associated large quantities of water only with inundation and death, was assembled on her diving-ledge, ready to admire and marvel.

The false modesty which had bothered her at first no longer troubled her as she slid off her clothes. Neither men nor women of the pygmies wore clothes in the ordinary course of things, and she knew now that they regarded hers not as a concealment, but as a badge of office. Her unclothed body they regarded with completely detached admiration. It looked, one of them had told her, as if there were light in it; white, but an utterly different white from the dead pallor of their own skins. For herself, she dreaded the time which must come when this translucence should thicken from lack of sunlight and air to an opaque chalkiness.

She stood for a moment, a slim figure poised on the brink, while the watchers held an awed silence. Then up and out. Her arms spread in the grace of a perfect swallow. She cut the water twenty feet below with the merest spurting of a splash.

For a time she entertained them, laughing up at faces which could not banish all traces of apprehension. She turned and twisted as she would, flashing her white limbs in the dark water. She let herself sink and swam twenty yards under water, baffling them agreeably as to her direction. An excited ovation greeted her reappearance—she had performed a near-miracle. At length she headed with a long, reaching crawl for the landing-place.

An elderly pygmy, whose face contrived to appear wrinkled while giving an impression of being tightly stretched across his skull, joined her on the march back to her cave. He was distinguished by wearing a garment. Not an elegant garment, for it was roughly woven from narrow strips of fungus skin, and fashioned into a very brief tunic, but it served to set him apart from his fellows. Margaret greeted him as 'Garm'—to the end she was never quite certain whether this was a name or a title, but it did what was needed. He responded by asking after her health perfunctorily, and after that of Bast with greater concern. She answered briefly, knowing that he would talk no more until her cave was reached and the guards were out of hearing.

With Garm alone of the pygmies was she able to hold conversations. Once she had learned enough of the language to make herself clear, she had determined to learn more of the people, but from most her questions met only rebuffs. Occasionally they called forth angry replies; more usually, they were disregarded in such a manner as to show that the inquiries were in bad taste if not indelicate. They made allowances for her infringements of their lesser taboos—after all, was she not privileged as the attendant of a goddess?—but became surly when she overreached certain mysteriously placed bounds of decency. Their displeasure was not infrequent. Safe passage along the catwalk of one's own racial code must be achieved through long experience; it is harder still to climb from it to another, and when that other is as involved as a maze and is entirely supported by incomprehensible misconceptions, a foot is bound to slip through the fabric from time to time. Margaret did her best to step warily after the first gross blunders, but it was not easy.

Garm was different from the rest. It is the stupid who become more bigoted with age, and Garm was not stupid. In his world he was a wise man who saw many inconsistencies in his people's beliefs. His complacency had been early upset by theories which snapped from rotten roots, and he had begun to keep a watch for flaws upon which he nurtured a growing tolerance. Impious unorthodoxies appeared in his mind, clinging like lichens to its barrenness, finding nourishment scarce, yet surviving. Many youthful precepts and implanted conceptions had withered down to the stalks; only a hardy few now showed good foliage; fewer still were entirely untouched by the blight of inquiry.

All his life he had hidden his doubts, partly from fear, more from policy. Why should he show them? Either they would upset the established order of things, or else, and more likely, he would suffer punishment. Neither would be of the slightest use. Probably he would meet the usual fate of heretics, and he would have accomplished nothing but death for the sake of a very little knowledge.

He wanted to know more. The desire to learn had been the heaviest fetter on his tongue, and he was glad now that he had held his peace. The odds and ends of information he had gained from this woman prisoner were in parts wise, trivial, or absurd. A few fitted into his jigsaw of beliefs, many were useless. But they were all interesting and new—perhaps he was the only man of his race to show interest in the new; he had never met another.

Conversation between the two was not easy. It was not enough that he had taught her his language. There were so many things in her life which were not in his, many words which whole sentences of his language failed to explain, so that he had perforce to learn something of hers. They talked now, and wallowed through swamps of misunderstanding in a mixture of the two.

Back in the cave, Margaret's first concern was with Bast. As long as the cat lived she was safe. Should it die, she did not know what might happen. Had she been sure that such an event would ensure her banishment to the prison caves, Bast's career would have been short. But the pygmies held a belief in survival after death; a belief which they inconveniently extended to include animals. It was quite on the cards that she might be despatched to attend the cat on its journey through the shades. Cautious inquiry of Garm, who still retained views on the divinity of cats, did nothing to dispel this notion. After all, he pointed out, a sacred cat could scarcely be left to shift for itself, and who could be better suited to attend it than those who had looked after it in life? It might resent having strangers thrust upon it and be displeased with those who had sent them. A wise man tried to please even the whims of a goddess. Granting feline immortality, it all sounded uncomfortably logical. To Margaret, doubting any kind of immortality save that vicariously achieved through offspring, it was doubly vexing.

She examined the cat and made certain that it would take some time to chew through the present cord. Never again should Bast escape if she could help it; there had been more than enough trouble last time. Assured of its safety, she brought a small bowl from the corner. Bast looked at the contents, sniffed with that reserve common to cats, and began to eat with no reserve whatever.

There had been some preliminary dietetic difficulties. Bast had firmly refused fungus food in any form. Margaret in a series of pictures which had excited general admiration, had succeeded in making the fact clear to the pygmy mind. This got them only a little farther, since it seemed that food and fungi were synonymous. Milk? But one could not draw a picture of milk. She tried her hand at a cow. It was not a success. Not only was it a bad picture of the 'square-animal-with-a-leg-at-each-corner' variety, but it rested very heavily upon a religious corn. Only later, when she saw carvings of Hathor, did she realise that she had been on dangerous ground.

She thought again. What did cats eat? Of course, fish. This time enormous discussion was provoked. According to Garm's subsequent explanation, a question of precedence had arisen. Was it legitimate to feed the symbol of Bast upon the symbols of Hamhit? This embraced the practical question of which goddess had the more powerful means of advertising her displeasure—for one of them must be displeased, since either cat or fish must die. The puzzle was at length solved by the suggestion that there were many fish to be had, but only one cat. Hamhit might not grudge (or not miss) a few.

They had brought them. Unpleasant monstrosities caught in the subterranean rivers, and unlike any Margaret had ever seen. White and eyeless, born of a million generations blind in the darkness. One eel-like creature among them found particular favour with Bast.

Reassured by the cat's appetite, she could now turn to her own food. She had grown used to the monotonous diet, and was able to eat the mess of chopped fungi with much the same indifference as she would have taken bread at home. Garm sat down near her, dipped a stone cup into a bowl of spirit and sipped from it. The bowl was there for his particular benefit. Margaret had tried the stuff once only; she classified it several stages below that inferior vodka which is made from bread. Garm evidently enjoyed it; he took several sips before settling down to resume 'yesterday's' broken conversation. His particular interest at the moment centred in the treatment of animals. Though his experience of them was limited to a few cats, dogs, rats, and other small creatures which had somehow found their ways below, he knew of others from pictures and carvings.

Preliminary misunderstandings had been lessened by now. Margaret had succeeded in dispelling the idea that a cow consisted of a bovine head mounted upon a female human torso. The old man found this revolutionary, but not incredible; he had already been troubled by the difference between a live dog and the classical figure of Anubis.

'You do not worship animals?' he asked.

'No,' Margaret said. 'At least, not in our country,' she amended.

'And the gods are not angry?'

'I don't think so. You see, ours are different gods.'

Garm considered the point. The idea of gods unassociated with animals was difficult, but he managed it.

'Then, since you are not afraid of the gods and the animals must eat much food, why do you not kill all those animals you do not wish to eat?'

'We make them work for us.'

'But you talked of special metal creatures you had made to work for you—far stronger than men or animals.'

'Yes, but for some things it is cheaper to employ animals than machines.'

Garm looked wonderingly at Bast.

'And what do cats do for you?'

'They catch mice.'

'What are mice?'

Margaret groaned privately and started to explain. That was always the trouble with these conversations. There were so few points of contact that everything was continually being interrupted by the most trivial explanations. Moreover, she was tired of the status of animals, and wanted to change the subject. But that was not Garm's way; he got his teeth into a topic, and worried at it. Soon he succeeded in finding out, to his great satisfaction, that there was a class of animals, known as pets, which did no work, and, furthermore, that a society for protecting the rights of animals was upheld chiefly by the supporters of these parasites. He seemed to regard this as the beginning of a return to grace.

'It shows,' he said, 'that they are beginning again to worship animals.'

'It doesn't—it shows sublimation,' Margaret objected.

Sublimation took some explaining, but he got it at last. Instead of resenting the idea, he welcomed it, and plunged forthwith into a number of incomprehensible statements about the relationship of religion with sublimation, from which he emerged with the idea of increasing animal worship somehow strengthened.

'They keep animals, pets, you call them, for no obvious reason. That means that they must find something in the animals which they cannot find elsewhere. That is the divine spirit. Knowing of this divine spirit, they band together into a noble society to preach it, so that others may recognise it.'

'No. You don't understand. There's nothing divine about it—in fact, they say that animals have no souls.'

Garm looked momentarily shocked by the heresy.

'But they live.'

'Of course, but our people say that only human beings have souls.'

'Why?'

Margaret was forced to admit that she did not know why. Garm became triumphant.

'It means that your people are beginning to regain faith. Soon they will admit that animals have souls. In their hearts they must know it already. If they did not, is it likely they would spend so much time and wealth upon animals?'

'Quite likely,' Margaret thought.

'No, you do not understand. I mean, if they thought animals to be soulless, they would obviously spend for the good of men whom they know to have souls. It would be waste to do otherwise.

'You say your world is in difficulties. It is not surprising, for you have spurned the gods. But now that their servants are once more being recognised, the gods will smile again upon you.'

'Oh,' said Margaret.

The idea of world redemption through the R.S.P.C.A. was novel, even if it inspired little faith.

Garm, with the status of animals settled to his satisfaction, became approachable on other subjects. She inquired for news.

'Have there been any more breaks?'

'No,' he told her. No more breaks, but two airshafts had had to be stopped when the water came trickling in.

So the New Sea was still rising. Margaret wondered how long the great pipes at Qabés would continue to pour out their millions of gallons. There had been no bad break for some little time, but it was an ever-present possibility. The weight of water was slowly and relentlessly finding out the weak spots, and driving through. So far they had beaten it by blocking the passages, but one by one the air inlets were being covered. How many of those hundreds of small fissures, which were the caves' natural ventilating system, could they spare before the air would thicken unbreathably? Each time that she heard that there was one less, it seemed to her that the caves became a little more stuffy. It looked like being a question which would deal the final blow, suffocation, or drowning?

The configuration of the caves puzzled her more than a

little. One 'day' she had managed to evade her guards, and had made her way back to the cavern where she and Mark had landed. She had stood at the top of the ramp and looked down on the *Sun Bird* still lying where Mark had moored her—how long ago? But the water no longer rushed through the cavern. The break had been blocked. Only a current so slight as scarcely to trouble the surface flowed across from the tunnel down which they had swept, to an opening on the opposite side. The cavern lake was now so smooth that reflection rivalled original.

Gazing down on the hull of the maimed *Sun Bird*, Margaret was tempted. It would be so easy just to run down the ramp, to jump aboard and cast off. Surely it would be better to drift away into that other tunnel and take one's chance, than to continue this existence among the pygmies. Probably she would fail, but what did that mean? Just to die a little earlier; to perish in the attempt rather than to wait here and drown. And she might have the luck to get free—to save this subterranean place and its people—and Mark. She imagined herself fighting officials, working night and day, pulling strings until at last the Qabés pumps should cease to turn. An expedition would be sent down to free Mark and the other inhabitants of the prison system.

For a long time she looked, but though her fancy soared, her body did not move. She was afraid, but that was not the whole cause of her hesitation—she was no more afraid to go than to stay. Another feeling held her back. A sensation that she might help here, that someone—Mark?—might need her, and she would have deserted. It would be all but impossible for her to escape alone, and by trying she might in some way wreck the chances of others. It was not very clear; but it was very compelling. With a sigh, she had turned away from the sight of the *Sun Bird*, and gone back to search for her distracted guards.

There had, she knew, been other breaks since the one which had engulfed Mark and herself, and yet there was the *Sun Bird* floating at practically the same level as before. It was puzzling. She decided to ask Garm about it, without revealing her reasons. At that time they had talked with difficulty, but as far as she could understand he had replied:

'The caves are on many levels. Often they are like a series of deep holes connected by passages. Only in those where the floors of the caverns to be connected are of even, or almost even depth, do the passages enter and leave at ground level. Often it has been more convenient to cut an entrance part way up a wall, and make a ledge sloping to the ground. Thus the actual tunnelling can be made shorter. Sometimes there have been fissures, and at others formations of harder rock to be avoided. There is no regularity. Therefore, it follows that although some of the breaks have sent water pouring down to the lowest levels, others have entered these well-like caves, and we have been able to stop them before they could reach the side passages and overflow. It is lucky that there are less of us than there were, for already all the lowest caverns are flooded deeply.'

With this she had to be satisfied, though it left much unexplained. Why, for instance, was there a slight current through the *Sun Bird*'s cave? Was it making its way to the pygmies' lower levels? If so, why hadn't they stopped it? The only other possibility seemed to be that the water was flowing beyond the pygmy system; that the incoming water had joined the course of a subterranean river already flowing through the cave. In the end she had sighed and given it up—one had to give up so many problems in this incomprehensible place.

It was a relief to know that there had been no more breaks lately. Each time she had heard of one her heart raced painfully, until she was sure that the prison caves had not been threatened. At first she had been angry with herself for her own anxiety—it rose, involuntary and unwanted. She had not yet forgiven Mark for the slaughter of the pygmies. It had been the sudden intrusion of violence which had shocked her even more than the violence itself. For a long time she had been unable to picture Mark without seeing those pathetically childlike bodies sprawling before him. Had she been able to reach the *Sun Bird* again before her first wrathful resentment had cooled, there would have been no hesitation to deter her.

Familiarity with the idea had now damped down the

sense of shock. Insensibly she had begun to adopt something of the pygmy attitude. The thing had happened. Lives had been lost; it was unfortunate, but it could not be helped. There was no demanding the blood of the slayer; no suggestion that he might have behaved differently. The pygmies seemed to attach less importance than did her own people to the act of dying. Or did they? Wasn't it rather that her people attached an exaggerated importance to the more sensational and spectacular forms of death? At home, more indignation and publicity was expended upon one murder (justified or not) than upon a hundred fatal road accidents. But death was just as final. Obviously then, it was the manner which counted, not the act; if it were not so, there would be no difference between hanging by the law, and hanging by private individuals, whereas everybody knows that the law may do many things which the private individual may not. Yes, it was the manner which stirred people's emotions. If you were to shoot a man because he was a public danger, everybody would be enraged, but if you killed an excellent citizen through negligent driving, nobody minded very much. It was all very confusing.... Anyhow, the emergent fact was that the pygmies did not draw these nice distinctions, they seemed to put all deceases under the heading of death from misadventure. Death, after all, was as natural as birth, all that had been done was to accelerate its advance. Everyone was condemned to death by being born, you couldn't change that.

As time went on the picture of the slain pygmies began to have less significance. They were no longer the shocking evidence of an unsuspected streak of brutality in Mark's nature.... At least, the idea of a streak of brutality was no longer shocking. In fact, there were things in favour of a streak (a narrow streak, of course) of brutality....

Garm broke in upon an interesting line of thought. The baffling time sense which the pygmies had evolved came into play as though an alarm clock had gone off in his mind.

'We must go now,' he interrupted.

Margaret had long ceased to be surprised by this bump of temporality. She rose, and crossed to Bast, gathering her up as she loosed the cord. Garm gulped down the dregs of his cupful of spirit, and led the way to the outer passage.

CHAPTER II

THE worship of Bast centred in one of the larger caverns. Immense labour had gone to make this place a fit dwelling for a goddess. The usual pygmy custom of smoothing only the most dangerous corners and cutting away the more obtrusive projections could not give a sufficiently polished effect for a divine sanctuary. The inconveniencies of rough adaptation might be good enough for themselves, but they were inadequate for a goddess. In pursuance of the axiom that good housing is more necessary for a bodiless spirit than for one's own flesh and blood, they had done their best. They had smoothed the rock walls almost to regularity before covering them with carvings in low relief. Broad bands of pictorial representation, alternating with narrower bands of purely conventional pattern now encircled the whole hall from floor almost to roof.

Margaret suspected that the broader bands contained a history, but, if so, it must have been designed for the edification of greatly gifted readers. Frequently the stiffness and angularity of the figures made them no more informative than the geometrical patterns above and below. Isolated groups in which battles—between slingers and stone-throwers—were taking place could be identified as could certain processions which might consist either of victors or vanquished; but the interdependence, if any, of these events was elusive.

Nor was Garm able to give any suggestions. The incidents, whatever they might be, were long forgotten, and the links between them entirely invisible. To him, and to all his race, the carvings were merely decoration. The knowledge of history had followed history itself into nullity. He knew only that they must have been made by his own people, since every figure was of pygmy cast. To this

Margaret's observation added that the eyes were set full face in profiles, after the Egyptian manner, and that the few colours used were applied sparingly, though with skilful effect. The main result of her inspection was to confirm her opinion that the race was now in an advanced stage of degeneracy.

At the far end of the cave stood a huge statue of the goddess, Bast; a concrete testimony of alien influence. The ponderous figure sat upon a throne. Straight-backed and dominant, she stared down the cave; great fists, set square upon the knees, held, one a sistrum, and the other, a shield. Further, to enhance its majesty, the sixty-foot sculpture had been mounted upon a dais of stone ten feet high. From the centre of the front panel a narrow flight of steps projected, leading up to an altar set between the gigantic feet.

Margaret never failed to be a little awed. Perhaps in the open, staring across Egyptian sands between the two immensities of desert and sky, the figure would have been unimpressive, but here, where confinement exaggerated, it all but overwhelmed. Only the face relieved its severity.

The sculptor, having flanked his work with twenty-foot images of cats, had been content that the goddess herself should show her humanity. Had he chosen to crown her with such a head as her two attendants wore, the effect would have been fearsome—as it was, he had given her a face in which wise benignity and peace went far to mitigate the sense of impotence which her size induced. To look up at it was to feel partially reassured. Its graven smoothness showed no trace of pygmy features. Margaret liked to think of it as the work of some captive more fortunate than herself; fortunate in that his faith had transcended his captivity. There were angles from which one could read into the stone face and the wide, calm eyes, compassion and, perhaps, a wistfulness as though something of the artist's exiled longing had survived in the stone.

As they entered, the crowd parted, leaving a straight, clear path between them and the steps. Garm fell back, allowing Margaret to take the lead. She paused for a moment, gazing up at the towering figure of Bast, then, keeping her eyes fixed upon the statue's face, she started forward with a slow dignity.

This was always the most trying part of the ceremony. The fact that she was, to pygmy eyes, clad in a robe of honour entirely failed to give her self-confidence. In her mind her grimy suit became even more grimy than in reality. At such a moment she longed for a skirt. There was grace and rhythm about a garment which hung; one could *move* in it. In breeches one seemed either strutting or striding; dignity was very hardly attained.

Pygmy heads to right and left bowed as she passed, offering homage not to her, but to the cat in her arms. Bast, with the detached superiority of cats, remained indifferent. She continued to purr loudly and contentedly.

The cave was more crowded than usual. Moreover, Margaret had the feeling that the crowd was expectant, not excited nor anxious, yet in a state where its members were stirred by one thought at the same time. This, in the stagnation of the caves, was sufficiently rare to be remarkable. She had known such simultaneity of emotion only a few times since her capture; on each occasion it had been traceable to the common danger from the water. But this time the reason did not serve; Garm had denied that there were any more breaks. Something else, of which she knew nothing, must be afoot. She was irritated by the sense that she was being kept out of things. Garm had let her down; after all, there was little enough to occupy one's interest in this place. A censorship would be intolerable....

At the head of the steps she halted, and set the cat down on the altar block. Her further duties as acolyte included only the fastening of the cord and a perfunctory bow of homage. Then she retired, leaving the stage to Garm.

From behind the idol's foot it was possible to look out past the curve of the great ankle bone, over the congregation. There was no doubt that it was far bigger than usual. Hundreds of silent pygmies—men, women, and children—stood motionless, listening to Garm's high-pitched intoning. For the most part their eyes followed the movements of the cat as it paced uneasily back and forth upon the block. The expressions of solemn awe which the creature produced had amused Margaret at first, but that had passed now. To all races the very rare is a matter either for awe or mirth. The very fact that life not unlike their own could take so different a shape, must be impressive to those who rarely, if ever, had seen an animal. There would be something magical about it—was there not always something magical about life? Was not her calm acceptance of it the result of being so much in contact with varied living forms? Familiarity with the miracle of existence had made it seem no miracle. To these people, knowing none of its forms save in themselves, their fungi crops and their fish, a simple cat became something occult. If one of the great stone cats beside the statue had come to life, and bounded from the block, they would have marvelled but little more. Margaret would have been far more startled than they. The cat in their eyes was a carving come to life, no wonder they were awed, no wonder they worshipped this goddess, Bast, who could breathe life, Pygmalion-like, into her symbols.

She turned her attention from the crowd to Garm. His speech was part prayer, and the prayer, like most prayers, part flattery. It was addressed to the cat as mediator between themselves and the goddess. The language, as in many primitive tongues, made great play with tonal variation, and the animal's restlessness was due mostly to the shrill sing-song aimed at it. Margaret's knowledge was sufficient to give her the general drift.

The goddess was implored to aid them. Surely they had deserved well by her? Had they not treated her symbol with all honour, risking even the displeasure of Hamhit for her sake? If anything which might have been done had been left undone, it was not by design, but through the ignorance of their inferior, contemptible minds. Of all the gods, Bast was the greatest, none in the whole celestial hierarchy could compare with her. Nor was the symbol of any other god so graceful, so detached, so calmly contemptuous of mere humanity. With the Ibis of Thoth they had held no truck (nor, indeed, with Thoth himself, for it ill became men to aspire to the wisdom of gods). The jackal of Anubis might await them among the shades, but Anubis was of little help in this life....

A disparagement of all the gods in glorification of Bast ensued. All, that is, with the notable exception of Ra. It was hoped, perhaps, that Bast might overlook this omission. Not even to curry her favour could the risk of sudden darkness be taken.

The prayer went on. A few pertinent remarks on the continued decline in the birth-rate were dropped in—'our fathers were multitudinous as the spores of a thousand mushrooms; they filled our caves from the lowest levels to the highest. We are but a remnant, shrunk and shrivelled, like a fungus in a dry place'—but still the main purpose of the speech remained hidden.

Margaret grew restive. Already the ceremony had lasted longer than usual. The cat tired of its prowling, and curled up comfortably in the middle of the altar. Garm's voice went on:

'—And now we implore that the blessing of Bast be given to our work. Though there may be destruction, yet it is ultimately to save, not to destroy, that we hope. Inasmuch as we have obeyed commands, that we have not wasted life by taking it wantonly, that we have imprisoned rather than slain, we ask help. Shall it ever be said that Bast has allowed ruin to be the consequence of obedience? We have faith that Bast will never forsake her people. Her justice, her mercy, her understanding, her ways inscrutable—these we honour. Will she not lend us now her wisdom, her wit, her power irresistible?'

Garm bowed low. The congregation knelt, and bent its faces to the floor. The old man's voice still muttered the sing-song prayer for blessings. His manner was less devout than that of the rest. One felt that he approached the goddess with a full knowledge of her obligations towards her people. There was an unmistakable air of 'we've done the right thing by you; now it's up to you not to let us down'. The conception of a bargain was blatant; almost put into words, though there was no threat of reprisals in case of Bast's default.

Margaret made one interesting discovery. She had wondered why the pygmies with their light regard of death troubled to imprison their captives. It now appeared as obedience to the goddess's direct wish. There was no humanitarian feeling behind it—merely blind observance of a religious rule. Had they been cramped for space, the law might have lapsed, as it was they were put to no trouble, since the captives were made self-supporting. She and Mark and all the prisoners probably had to thank the long dead Egyptian missionaries who had set up the temple for cunningly including a law for their own preservation in the articles of faith.

But still she had no clue to the reason for this special service. For all Garm's lack of humility, he showed far more supplication than was usual in his formal prayers.

She let her eyes rove over the hundreds of bowed, naked backs. Row upon row of them, white beneath the many globes, dull dry white; not one body with a healthy, gleaming skin. Her gaze reached the backmost row. Suddenly she stiffened, and leaned forward round the stone foot, staring fixedly. Her mouth opened, but she caught back the rising exclamation in time.

Beside the entrance stood a giant—at least, so he appeared to her first startled glance. She had grown so used to pygmy standards that it was hard to recognise him as a normal man. Her heart hammered with a sudden excitement, painfully so that she pressed a hand below her left breast. But it was not Mark. A sudden rush of dizziness, compound of shock and disappointment, left her leaning weakly against the stone. She forced her eyes back to the distant figure, and strained to distinguish the details. Absurd that she could ever have thought that it was Mark. This man was dark and bearded. His clothes, even, were unlike Mark's; he seemed to be wearing the rags of a uniform....

What could he be doing here? Why hadn't the pygmies captured him? It was impossible that anyone could have penetrated as far as this unseen.... Or had he escaped? No, that was obviously absurd. But wasn't his very presence here absurd? Garm had said that except for herself all the captives were in the prison caves—and once they were in, they stayed in. What, then——?

She gave it up, and stood watching him. He lounged against the wall; seemed to be watching with a kind of tolerant boredom. Evidently he stood in no fear of the pygmies. But why not?

Garm's prayer was ending. He was calling upon the concourse to proclaim the magnificence of Bast. The responses of their thin voices swept through the cavern like the rustle of a high wind.

Bast, the benign. Bast, the merciful. Bast, the omniscient.

The cat, disturbed, resumed its prowling. It mewed plaintively. Garm paused with both hands upraised; he knew something of the value of dramatic effect. In all the huge temple cave there was no sound but the thin crying of the cat.

The pygmies had gone, and Garm with them. Of all the hundreds who had filled the place only Margaret's four guards remained. But the stranger, the man at the far end, had not gone. He had stood close to the wall while the crowd passed out. They saw him, but they did not give him a second glance. Not until the last of them had been swallowed up in the tunnel did he rouse himself into an indolent saunter towards the statue. Margaret waited, watching his unhurried approach with a sense of misgiving. She had no premonition, merely a feeling that something was amiss. The man's casual air was unreasonably out of place in its surroundings.

He looked an unattractive specimen, but so, she reminded herself, would any man just free of the prison caves. The rags of his uniform dangled and flapped about him as he walked. The buttonless jacket fell open to show a hard muscled, though none too clean, chest and stomach. Beneath a tangle of black hair, dark eyes set in a sallow face were fixed on her own. The expression of his mouth was invisible behind a ragged scrub of beard and moustache.

His head tilted back as he looked up to the calm stone face far above. She saw a flash of white teeth as he smiled derisively. He began to mount the stairs without hesitation. Margaret shot a glance at her four guards. They were watching the man with the barest curiosity, certainly without animosity. He approached her where she stood beside the altar. For a moment his gaze was transferred to the cat. He put out a hand, and stroked it gently behind the ear. The expressions of the guards became respectful; it was evident that the man was on good terms with the goddess. The cat purred, and rubbed itself against his hand. Looking back to Margaret, he said:

'You've got a soft job, eh?' The English was easy

enough, but it was spoken with a strong Latin accent.

He looked her up and down in a fashion she did not like. It had the effect of making her feel far more naked than she had been when swimming to impress the pygmies. She tried to shake off the feeling of uneasiness he induced. It was ridiculous that she should feel like this towards the first man of her own kind she had seen for—how long?—well, a very long time.

'Who are you?' she asked.

'Miguel Salvades. And you are Miss Lawn?'

'How did you know?'

Miguel shrugged his shoulders.

'There is little news in the prison caves—when there is any, everybody knows it. When it is that a beautiful lady is imprisoned here instead of with the rest of us, everybody is very interested.'

'Then you have seen Mark? Tell me, how is he?'

'He is well now. He was very bad for a long time. They thought he would die.'

Margaret, too, had thought he would die. How those pygmies had hammered and beaten him! She had flung herself on them, trying to help, until others came and dragged her away. Her last sight of him had been of a battered and bleeding figure sprawling helpless on the ground. Only the repeated assurances of Garm had later convinced her that he had indeed survived that mauling.

'There've been no ill effects? Nothing broken?'

'He didn't look bad when I last saw him. Still weak, of course.'

Not until she had satisfied anxiety for Mark, did Margaret revert to the problem of this man's presence.

'How is it you are not a prisoner?' she asked.

'But I am. I've been in here more than four years.'

'No, I mean why are you here? How did you get out of the prison caves?'

'They let me out—they don't think I can do any harm.'

'Only you?'

'Yes, only me.'

Margaret frowned. Was he being deliberately evasive, or merely stupid? He didn't look stupid. She tried again.

'But why should they let you out? I thought they kept all prisoners in there always.'

'Except you? Yes, that is so. But I was able to do them a good turn. We made a bargain. They were to let me have the run of these caves if I did what they wanted.'

'And what was that?'

'Oh, just to give them some information.'

He uttered the last answer with an air of finality which discouraged further questions. Margaret found it irritating. Still, it was his own business. It was puzzling to know what information could have been important enough to support such a bargain. Such knowledge as she herself had tried from time to time to impart to the little people had never been welcomed with any enthusiasm. In any case, he had not gained a great deal. For herself, she would prefer to be in the prison caves with people of her own kind. She told him so.

'But I am not going to stay here. I'm going to escape.'

'How?'

He shrugged. 'I must look round—explore first. There are ways in—there must be ways out.'

She contemplated him, wondering how he proposed to escape. So far as she could see, it would be scarcely easier from here than from the prison caves. Openings there were, airshafts and cracks, hundreds of them, but the pygmies would be watching him just as they watched her. They might be a backward, simple race, but they were not fools. They must know why he had bargained for the freedom of the outer caves.

'Garm told me,' she said, 'that no one has ever got away.'

'I know, that's what they say, but . . . who is Garm?'

'The old man who was praying just now. He told me what happened to the last man who tried.'

'Well?'

'He started to climb an airshaft. They let him get a little way up, and then built a fire underneath—a big fire. The smoke and the heat were too much for him. He let go in the end, and came tumbling down. He landed in the fire, and they didn't bother to pull him out.'

'I see. They got rid of him, but no one could accuse them of actually killing him. Very nice.'

He appeared little perturbed by the prospect.

'Then you don't intend to try one of the airshafts?'

'I must look round,' he repeated. 'As I see it, there is no great hurry; a few days more or less doesn't count much on top of four years. It wants thinking out carefully. I must get out first time—there won't be a second chance.' He looked up and caught Margaret's doubting expression. 'Little ray of sunshine, aren't you?'

'What do you mean?'

'Well, all you've done up till now is to tell me how it's never been done, and can't be done. Anybody'd think you were in with these little devils.'

'I'm sorry, but—— You see, I thought of nothing but escape at first; then I found out it was hopeless. It's a bit difficult to get optimistic again suddenly. It's not even as if you had a plan. . . .'

'Maybe I have. I did manage to plan my way clear of the prison caves.'

'But you're just as much in prison now.'

He chose to ignore her last remark.

'You didn't try to make a break for it?'

Margaret shook her head. 'I thought of it once, but something held me back.'

'How do you mean?' Miguel looked puzzled.

'Just a feeling that if I did it, I'd be doing the wrong thing. An idea that I wouldn't get through, perhaps, and if I failed, I should have spoilt the possibility for anyone else.'

'I don't quite get you.'

'You heard how we got in?'

He nodded. 'In part of a wrecked plane, wasn't it?'

'Yes, and it's still there where we left it. There's a current running through the cave, but I don't know where it goes. I thought that if I went downstream for a bit I might get beyond the pygmy caves, and find a way out somewhere where they couldn't follow me. I know it all sounds rather vague—it wasn't really much of a plan; just an idea.'

'You think this river would carry you beyond the inhabited caves?'

'It might. It must go somewhere.'

Miguel did not answer at once, he seemed sunk in thought.

'It's only really necessary for one person to get out,' she

went on. 'Once this place is known about they'll send an expedition, and rescue us all. If you or I——' She looked at him, hesitating. After all, why not? Fear that she would be physically too weak to make good her escape had been the real deterrent. Miguel was far from weak. His was the hard, wiry type which could survive hardships. Why shouldn't he take a risk in the *Sun Bird*? He received the suggestion none too kindly.

'You'd rather I took the risk than you?'

'No, it's not that—I told you I don't think I could manage it.'

Miguel's attitude remained unenthusiastic. But in his eyes there was a gleam which Margaret missed.

'Don't you see?' she continued. 'It's the very chance you want. The pygmies don't know the *Sun Bird*'s there. They'd be puzzled right from the beginning. While they were looking for you in the airshafts, you'd be floating off miles away. You must take it—it's your one chance—our one chance.'

But Miguel continued to look dubious.

'How do I know I'll be able to find a way out?'

'You don't, but isn't it worth the risk? Oh, please, please try it—we're all depending on you; all those people down in the prison caves. If only you can do it, you'll save not only yourself, but all of us.'

'But how can I find this *Sun Bird*? Where is it?'

'I can't describe the way to it, but I can show you.'

Miguel was looking half convinced. He glanced doubtfully at the guards.

'We'll have to get rid of them.'

'I can dodge them—I did it before in one of the fungus caves.'

'When can we go?' Miguel spoke suddenly in a sharper tone. 'Now?'

Margaret hesitated. Why not now? They could take a circuitous route, give the guards the slip on the way.

'Yes,' she decided.

She picked up the cat, and turned towards the steps. At the top of the flight she halted suddenly. Garm had returned with several followers. Hastily she turned back to caution Miguel.

'Be careful with Garm, he knows some English.' She

made a quick decision. 'It's no good now. We couldn't shake them all off. Some other time.'

She turned to face the old man. He did not look pleased at the sight of Miguel, but he said nothing. Margaret wondered if he guessed that they had been talking of escape. Probably he did; it was the most likely topic.

She descended to meet him. His greeting was a shade curter than usual. The final glance he gave to Miguel was anything but friendly. Miguel grinned. As they passed away from him down the long temple, his grin grew broader.

He seemed oddly cheerful for one whose chance of escape had been delayed....

CHAPTER III

THE arrangement of a meeting in a place where opportunities are few, and time has no meaning, is not easy. As far as Margaret could discover, only four things in the caves proceeded with reliable regularity: her own sleeping periods, the worship of Bast, the ripening of the fungi, and the duration of the period of gestation. Since the last two were useless for the purpose of time fixing, and the first was a law to itself, phased with complete independence of externals, it became necessary to plan the meeting with reference to Bast. And even there difficulties arose. Ever since Garm's demand for the goddess's assistance, the smooth running of pygmy life had been disturbed. An air of activity and purpose, wholly foreign, was pervading the caves. Attentions to Bast were more frequent, more flattering and a little briefer.

It was four 'days'—judged in terms of her own sleeping—before she and Miguel met again. Had it been only one, or even two 'days' the course of events might have been very different. As it happened, Miguel found himself facing a woman who looked at him with a new and discouraging expression.

Margaret had been talking with Garm. Two unusual happenings in quick succession—the special prayer to

Bast, and the unhindered wandering of Miguel—had roused in her a curiosity which must be satisfied. Garm had explained. The new light in which he placed Miguel was not flattering. It threw shadows of other doubts. Had Miguel really been so unwilling to use the *Sun Bird* for escape? Had he been disarming suspicion by letting the suggestion come from her?

Perhaps she was misjudging him in that. If he had come openly and said that he wanted the *Sun Bird,* would she have refused it? She did not think so. Then why had he not done that? She tried to put herself in his place, but failed. It was scarcely surprising, for Miguel's was one of those minds which instinctively distrusts the obvious, preferring to hide even the simplest actions under an indirect method.

At this second meeting he noticed the look on her face with misgiving. She had found out something, then. But how much? Better let her tell him. Most likely he would put his foot in it if he spoke first.

'So you got here by giving away your friends?' she began. Miguel's face maintained an irritating blankness.

'You told the pygmies about their tunnel, didn't you?'

'Who said that?'

'I asked Garm why you were allowed here, and he told me.'

'You believe that little monkey?'

'I do.'

Miguel gave a snort of contempt.

'What other lies did he tell you?'

Margaret disregarded the question; she stared at him coldly.

'If that was not your side of the bargain, what was?'

'So you're open to believe what every little swine of a pygmy tells you, eh?'

'What did you do?' she repeated. Miguel's eyes fell.

'Yes, I told them,' he admitted at last.

'That was a pretty low down trick to play on your friends.'

'They were no friends of mine; they were working on their own.'

'But for your good. If they had made the tunnel it would have meant your freedom as well as theirs.'

'If they'd made their tunnel,' he laughed. 'As if they'd ever make their damned tunnel. Why, do you know how long they had been working on it? Years, and others for years before that. They'd never have got it through, the fools. Sweating their guts out over a job which would never be any good to anyone.'

'So you felt justified in throwing away all those years of work by telling the pygmies?'

'Well, who wouldn't for a chance?'

Margaret looked at him with contempt.

'A chance. You chuck away all their work to get here without even a plan of getting any farther. Just hoping for a bit of luck.'

'You're wrong there. I did have a plan.'

'Yes, to get hold of the *Sun Bird*. Why couldn't you tell me that right out?'

Miguel looked momentarily disconcerted.

'You wouldn't have agreed.'

'Yes, I should, but I'm doubtful now.'

'You——?' Miguel frowned.

'What'll you do if you get out? You've let your friends down once.... I very much doubt whether it's worth risking.'

Margaret was speaking rhetorically. She had no intention of withdrawing the offer of the *Sun Bird* but she had begun to dislike Miguel heartily. He however, took the threat seriously, it frightened him.

'What do you mean? I've got to have it. Do you think I'm going to rot in this lousy hole on account of you? The sooner you lead me to it, the better it'll be for you.'

He glared at her in sudden panic. It was in her power to upset all his plans; to keep him imprisoned here for the rest of his life. It would have been wiser to strike a more submissive note, but his alarm had taken him by surprise.

The counterpart of his frown appeared on Margaret's face. She was unafraid of him, and of his scowls, but she was surprised by the peremptory tone. It was wrong in the circumstances, the kind of outburst one expected from a cornered man, not from one going on a mission of rescue. Nor was she aware of all his misgivings. For one thing, he was not as easy about the pygmies as he pretended. Once they had closed the tunnel, they might take it into their heads to send him back to the prison caves. That would not be pleasant. His own friends whom he had left directing the pygmy forces would not welcome him for throwing away his chance, nor would the revenges of Smith, Ed, and the rest be gentle. Miguel was gifted with an uncomfortably good imagination concerning nastinesses. Then, too, there was the possibility of a pygmy defeat. Suppose the prisoners broke out! Suppose Zickle or one of the others came hunting him through the tunnels! The idea made him sweat. He must have the *Sun Bird,* and get clean away from all of them. He continued to glare savagely at the girl—he was more used to the positions of the sexes reversed. She said calmly:

'And when you get out?' He looked blank. She continued: 'What are you going to do then? Where are you going to lay information?'

Miguel's reply was vague and unsatisfactory. It sounded lame in his own ears. He ought to have thought up some convincing details. Damn the woman! Margaret allowed him to stumble through.

'So you'd never thought of it,' she said cuttingly as he finished. 'Perhaps you never intended to think of it? It seems to me you're just out to save your own miserable skin—you don't care if the rest of us die here.'

Since this was precisely Miguel's attitude, his protests, though vigorous, were unconvincing. He became more angry; partly with Margaret; partly with himself. He ought to have settled the whole thing last time—in fact, he had considered it settled. Never for a moment had he thought that she might get the whole yarn out of Garm. But for all that, he was irritatingly aware that he might have saved himself had he handled this second talk better.

Of course, she was right—he hoped the rest would rot here. Miguel had never yearned for publicity. If he were to succeed in convincing the authorities of the existence of the pygmies (not an easy matter in itself), he would be in the glare of a veritable floodlight of publicity. Various persons who had been industriously seeking him for years would immediately find him—with fatal consequences. In the all too likely event of his story being disbelieved, he would be sent to the penal battalion as a deserter from the Legion. He had had enough of the Legion proper; the idea of the penal battalion made him feel sick. He'd heard some stories.... No, either way it was a poor look-out. All he wanted to do was to re-emerge into the world in the least obtrusive fashion possible.

Margaret was convinced by now that he intended to do nothing to help them. He could see by her face that she believed no word of his protestations. Her mouth was set in an obstinate line. She knew that once he got the *Sun Bird* they would hear no more of him. Miguel saw that he had gone too far; he allowed his anger to die down, and changed his tactics.

'You don't believe me,' he accused bitterly.

'Not a word,' Margaret agreed.

He was desperate; there was still a chance.

'Why don't you come, too?' he began.

Margaret's first impulse was to disregard the suggestion, but as he continued, she began to wonder. He explained his own difficulties honestly and truthfully. His attitude became for the first time comprehensible. Without any doubt contact with the authorities would put him between the devil and the deep sea.

'But for you, it is different,' he pointed out. 'You can raise hell with the English and the French, and get everyone out.'

The idea tempted. The more she thought of it, the better it seemed. When (and if) they got out, Miguel could disappear, and leave her to make the report. The difficulties which had daunted her before would be diminished by the presence of a companion, and even if she failed, she would at least have tried. The real objection was Miguel himself. He was so slimy. He twisted and turned when there was no need. Why couldn't he have told her before that he was afraid of the authorities? It seemed impossible to trust him an inch. There was no doubt that he had betrayed his companions in the prison caves, and equally little doubt that he would betray anyone else, should he think it to his advantage.

With the temptation came a weighty sense of responsibility. Unless something were done soon, it would be too late. No one could tell when there might be a break which would flood the whole system. On the other hand, if Miguel was up to some new trick, it might ruin the last hope. He was still urging, but she scarcely heard him. She had no intention of being driven to a hurried decision. She must think it out.

The procrastination sent Miguel almost frenzied. He cursed, argued, and threatened, but Margaret remained adamant; she must have time.

She walked out with her four guards, leaving him trembling in a fury of exasperation.

CHAPTER IV

LITTLE of Margaret's next 'night' was spent in sleep. Mostly she lay restless, turning the problem round and round to examine each facet. Her mind felt weighted down with liability; it could move only sluggishly instead of jumping.

The *Sun Bird* she had now come to regard as the essential fulcrum of escape; to waste it would be to lose everything. Had the escaper been anyone but Miguel, she would not have hesitated to go with him—or even to let him go alone. But that did not help. Miguel was Miguel, and no amount of wishing would change him. Why, out of all the hundreds of men in the prison caves, must it be Miguel who had escaped? The answer was obvious. If it had not been Miguel, it would have been someone like him. The essence of his ability to get so far lay in that very fact. Only someone utterly unprincipled and ruthless could have made that bargain with the pygmies.

And if he had been ruthless once, why not again? He was already angry with her. Why should he keep his part of the bargain when there was nothing to hold him to it? It would be only too easy for him once they had started to push her overboard and let her drown.

Margaret turned uneasily. Yes, that would be child's play. Just the sort of satisfactorily complete ending to the affair which would please a mind like Miguel's. She could see just how he would look at it: This woman might tell the authorities of him either by accident, or by citing him as a witness to the truth of her story. Why take chances?

Settle her out of hand, and stop any possibility of trouble.

And then...? Not only would she have lost her life, but the *Sun Bird* would be gone too....

Wasn't there some way of getting a hold on Miguel to force him to keep the bargain?

Money? A good round sum to be paid over when she should reach safety.... But she had very little money. Mark had plenty, she knew, but that was not much good. For one thing he might not fulfil a promise made by her to Miguel, and, for another, the chances of his rescue alive were problematical. So much so that they could scarcely be expected to restrain Miguel if he thought himself in jeopardy. No, money would not serve. What would?

Her thoughts swept round in overlapping circles. They multiplied; their pattern grew more intricate, more mazy, but they led nowhere. Not in a single place did the line of argument shoot off to form a plan. She grew wearied of the infinite revolutions, and dragged herself back to the single fixed point of the pattern. It all hinged on one question.

Was she, or was she not justified in risking the *Sun Bird* with such a man as Miguel?

Put like that, the answer was obvious. She was not.

And on that decision she went to sleep.

She told Garm about Miguel the next 'day'. It was not an agreeable task. Her betrayal of him seemed from some points of view to drag her down to his own level. But she made herself do it. If the safety of the *Sun Bird* was as important as she had assumed, it must be assured at all costs. Miguel might succeed in finding it without her help; he might be searching for it even now. And he must be stopped. Suppressing any reference to the *Sun Bird,* she set herself to blacken, if possible, Miguel's character.

Garm listened willingly. His original dislike of Miguel, founded not on the other's underhand methods so much as on pure prejudice, made him a good subject. He was not vastly surprised to hear of the projected escape; that was only to be expected, and not very worrying—in fact the sooner it occurred, the sooner this Miguel business would be settled. When he was told, however, that it was proposed that Margaret should accompany the flight, his indignation rose. To attempt one's own freedom was natural, but to suggest such a course to the hand-maiden of a goddess was vile.

And that was not all. With rising anger he listened to a well-coloured account of Miguel's attentions and intentions towards her. By the end of it Margaret had succeeded in rousing him to a remarkable state of fury. Garm himself set little prize on celibacy, but he was convinced that the goddess insisted upon virginity in her chief attendant. But there was worse to follow. It appeared that this scum, this filth, this Miguel had profaned holiness, had committed such coarse sacrilege as revolted the mind, had outraged the spirit of the goddess at her very shrine, had, in fact, spat in the cat's eye.

Garm swept from the cave in a passion, leaving Margaret a little stunned by her success. That afterthought had done more than all the rest. She looked across at Bast, who blinked solemnly back at her.

'It's lucky you can't let me down,' she told her. 'That's certainly finished Miguel, and you seemed rather fond of him. Scratched your ears nicely, didn't he?'

She was suddenly struck by a spasm of remorse. Had she pitched it too strong? Even though she hated him, she had no wish for his death upon her conscience. Garm had looked too angry to stop at mere detention, but she hoped he would. After all, Miguel had wanted freedom no less than the rest. His weapons had been base, but he had no others. One should not blame him too much....

Resolutely she put the subject away. She had considered it her duty, and whatever happened now was outside her control.

She took one of the white, eyeless fish from a bowl and began to cut it up with a sharp stone for Bast. The cat still seemed to thrive; that was a blessing. She put the fragments into a smaller bowl, and pushed it across the floor. It was odd the extent to which events had depended upon that bundle of fur.

But for it, she would have been in the prison caves. It was because she was here and able to show him the way to the *Sun Bird* that Miguel had made his bargain—for she was sure now that he had intended from the beginning to get hold of it. Because of that bargain a war was now going on in the prison caves. Her thoughts drifted to Mark. Would he be strong enough yet to fight? What sort of fighting could it be? No firearms, no swords even. A hand to hand tussle, she supposed. The pygmies had been greatly thinned by the numbers drafted away. Since the special prayers to Bast, which she now recognised as the send-off of the expeditionary force, the attenders at the temple meetings had been mostly women.

And the prisoners had beaten off the first attack. Garm had told her that with mingled sorrow and surprise. His pride of race had been hurt. On the purely practical grounds of size it was only to be expected that one of the prisoners should be a match for two pygmies, but when a mere hundred and fifty or so were able to defy well over a thousand pygmies, he felt humiliated. He understood it to be due to guile.

'We,' he explained, 'are honest fighters. We fight with pride in our skill and our strength, but these prisoners....' He shook his head. 'They do not know how to fight. They work with cunning and hidden subtleties, instead of fighting like men with sling and knife. It degrades warfare....

'Of course'—he became magnanimous—'they can scarcely be blamed. They have not our standards. Coming, as they do, from a world which has forsaken the gods so that devils may stalk in spurious honour, it is not surprising that they have learned meannesses of spirit, unworthy stratagems which we despise.'

'We have a saying,' Margaret told him, apologetically, 'that all's fair in war.'

Garm looked shocked.

'Truly you have some remarkable sayings—I think this is the worst you have told me yet. Is there no honour in your wars?'

'Very little. Though you would find many people to agree with you, that the more subtle and drastic weapons should be abolished.'

'They know they are dishonourable, then? There is some hope for you.'

'No, that's not quite right. You see, they don't think of war in terms of honour, any more.'

'Then why do they want them abolished?'

'They think they are too dangerous.'
'They are cowards?'
'No.'
'But they must either be cowards or men of honour.'
'They're men of sense, up to a point.'
'But have you no men who think of the glory of war?'
'Oh yes; but they're mostly very young—too young to have had any experience of it. They are the ones who talk about all being fair in war.'
Garm appeared confused.
'Do you mean that the men who will use all guile, every cunning means to destroy their enemies, are the same who believe in the honour of war?'
'They are about the only ones,' Margaret agreed.
'But that is absurd. How can it be honourable to fight with tricks? Skill, yes, but tricks, no.'
'But what you call tricks, they call skill,' she attempted patiently.
'No,' said Garm, 'not even such a race as yours could sink as low as to confuse tricks with skill. It is that you are a woman, and do not understand these things. The female mind——'
Margaret hastily headed him back to the subject of the war. She had heard Garm on the female mind before.
'But what are your men going to do? Will they retire?'
'Retire?' Garm looked horrified.
'But if your attacks can be repulsed?'
'They have repulsed us once. We shall change our plan.'
'Trick them?'
'Certainly not. We shall merely adopt other methods. We never trick. When we fight an enemy who knows nothing of honour, we adapt—temporarily, of course—our methods to his. We do not approve, but self-defence demands it.'
'There seems to be something familiar about that,' said Margaret.
The conversation had revealed an unexpected side of pygmy activities. Garm's 'when we fight' had surprised her inasmuch as there appeared to be no one for them to fight. She inquired:
'When did you last fight?'

But Garm could not tell. There had been no fighting in his own time. Nevertheless, tradition spoke of expeditions from time to time against the prisoners, and more than one civil war between the devotees of rival gods. In any case, he insisted, these wars had always been fought in an honourable way. It was because this particular *fracas* was being conducted in such an undignified manner that it had been necessary (against their better standards) to call in all available help.

The 'natives' had been willing to co-operate since the caves were as much home to them as they were to the pygmies. And certain of Miguel's friends had joined them—though whether this was done on the principle of backing the winners, or as a result of bribery, she was unable to discover—they were supplying the guile which the high-minded pygmies naturally lacked. Garm's attitude towards them was a mixture of admiration of their ingenuity, with contempt for their standards. There was no word for serpent in the pygmy tongue; if there had been, he would undoubtedly have used it to describe the renegades.

Margaret's final deduction was that the besieged prisoners were holding their own, and likely to do so for some time to come. As long as the fighting went on Miguel was certain of the freedom of the outer caves, and at liberty to search for the *Sun Bird*. The more she considered it, the more glad she was to have put a spoke in his wheel.

But the apprehension of Miguel did not proceed smoothly. In answer to her worried questions, Margaret's guards could tell her nothing more than that the order had gone out for his capture. She was forced to wait until Garm's next visit. When he came, it was with a gloomy face.

No. Miguel had not been caught yet. He had disappeared. Hidden himself in the disused galleries and caves where it would be difficult to find him. No one living knew the geography of those parts, though once upon a time, when the pygmies had been as numerous as the spores in a thousand puff-balls—Margaret listened patiently again to a repetition of past glories. She became uncomfortably aware that she had not been justified in dismissing Miguel from her mind.

'But surely,' she interrupted, 'they will be able to hunt him down soon.'

'Of course.' Garm spoke with a confidence which his earlier remarks scarcely vindicated. Though he might believe his people to be mistaken on some points, and misinformed on others, yet his pride in them was immense. The idea of the pygmies failing to do anything they chose to take up was completely foreign to him. Even their inability to deal with the gradual flooding had shaken his faith only slightly—deep down, he was sure that they would come through this peril as they had come through others. As to this matter of one escaped prisoner, it was unthinkable that he could evade them for long. The real cause for worry was lest the goddess should be angered by delay in the blasphemer's punishment. An expedition must be sent to search the disused caverns, and he had not at present many men to spare.

'Does he know you want him?' Margaret asked.

Garm nodded. 'It is unfortunate. We found the bodies of two of the men who were sent to find him. Their slings and knives had gone.'

'You're sure he killed them?'

'Who else?'

'Then he must know.'

Margaret's misgivings grew. The thought of the unscrupulous Miguel further goaded by desperation increased her uneasiness almost to fear. For the first time she was thankful for the continual presence of her four guards. Miguel could have little doubt who had started the hunt. It would not be pleasant to meet him alone.

'It was foolish,' Garm was saying. 'The men should have worked in fours, not in pairs. We have lost time now that he is warned.' He glanced across at Bast, curled up into a rythmically expanding and contracting ball. 'She is well?' he asked anxiously.

'Quite well.'

Garm was relieved. It was lucky that there had been no manifestations of the goddess's displeasure as yet. But the matter must not be allowed to slide. An uneasy thought struck him—there had been a second defeat in the prison caves; the tactic of advancing behind mushroom heads had been out-manoeuvred; was it not possible that Bast was showing her resentment in this way?

The more he considered it, the more likely it appeared. He wondered why he had not thought of it before. Nothing but divine opposition could have wrecked so subtle a move as that second attack. How could he have been so foolish as to think that she would fail to act? What goddess worth her salt would remain passive while her symbol was made a target for expectoration? The sooner atonement was made, the better for everyone. Miguel must be found without delay. In his sharpened urgency, the old man left the cave almost at a run.

Margaret was left with a shadow on her spirit. She pictured Miguel prowling through passages and caverns, hunting for the *Sun Bird*. Or would he be keeping to the disused parts to evade pursuit? Would even a man of Miguel's type wait to be ferreted out as he must be, sooner or later? It was more to be expected that desperation would make him reckless. However, that had its better aspect. The odds against his finding the *Sun Bird* before he fell in with search parties of pygmies were immense.

Gradually Margaret worked herself into an easier frame of mind. She saw in their true proportions the obstacles she had managed to raise between a single, unassisted man and his desire. If he should succeed, it would be by the merest fluke. She had done her best.

She yawned wearily. How long, she wondered, since she had slept? It felt like bedtime again, anyhow. She loosened her clothes and lay down, looking up at the glowing light. How many years did it take to adapt oneself to this nightless existence? Without day and night as measures, one never seemed fully awake or asleep, but spinning out a monotonous existence somewhere in between the two. Now, to Bast it didn't matter a bit; provided she was fed frequently, she seemed prepared to doze the rest of the time. Margaret wished, not for the first time, that she were like that....

Her eyes were still enviously on the cat when the lids slipped over them....

CHAPTER V

MARGARET was awakened by a half-heard sound from the corridor outside. Nothing very unusual in that. Her inability to fit her 'nights' into the pygmy time-scheme had led more than once to Garm's having to wake her for the temple ceremonies. When and where the pygmies slept she did not know, but she suspected that it was in short spells of two or three hours at frequent intervals.

She lay for some moments without moving, her eyes on the entrance; but the old man did not appear. She called out in the pygmy language:

'What do you want?'

There was no answer. She raised herself on one elbow.

'Guards?'

Still no answer. Only a faint sound of movement in the passage. Margaret got up and crossed to look out. Something must be wrong; the guards had never before failed to answer her. The six-foot passage between her cell and the main corridor was empty. But at the end, protruding beyond the left-hand corner, was a naked foot with toes pointing up into the air. She could see all the lower part of the leg as far as the knee, lying motionless. She spoke again, but still there was no reply. Queer, why didn't one of the other guards speak? They wouldn't all be asleep. She stepped forward, keeping her eyes on the foot. She put her head round the corner, and stared down at a body on the floor. It was one of her guards, and he was very dead. His head was savagely battered, a lot of blood and other things had spilt on the floor. Margaret opened her mouth, but before the cry could come, a pressure, rigid as steel, fastened on her throat.

Both her hands flew up, wrenching and scratching at the sinewy fingers which were strangling her. Her nails filled with skin from them, but they did not loosen; her fingers could find no hold to prise them apart. She lowered her right arm, and sent back the elbow in a vicious jab. It met something yielding and brought forth a sudden grunt, the grip was cruelly increased till her head felt as if it would burst from the pressure of pounding blood.

She felt herself whirled round, and forced back to her cell.

On her bed of fungus skin strips she was thrust face down. Only then did the terrible grip on her throat relax. She could not cry out nor struggle; she could do nothing but draw a deep breath into lungs which ached for the lack of it. The respite was brief; a weight—a knee, she guessed—was thrust on the back of her neck, crushing her face among the fibres so that again she could scarcely breathe. Hands groped for her arms; found them, and tied the wrist tightly together with a coarse cord which cut deep. There was a fumbling, followed by a ripping sound as the back of her silk shirt was torn away. Then she was twisted over, and the silk bound tightly over her gasping mouth.

Miguel rose to his feet, and looked down at her. He raised a bleeding hand, and licked clean the scratches her nails had left.

'Wild little bitch!' he said venomously. 'Now it's my turn. Thought you'd finished with me, didn't you? Told the little devils a whole pack of lies about me. I'll make you eat 'em. I'll make you sorry you ever lived to tell 'em—you dirty little double-crosser.'

A faint sound came from the far corner. Miguel spun round to face Bast in the performance of her usual awakening yawn. She looked up at him and mewed.

'Told them I'd spat in its eye, did you? Well, see what I really do.'

He jumped towards it and seized it by the tail. It gave one screech, which was cut short as its head met the wall. Miguel dropped the body and turned back to glare at Margaret.

'And as for what's going to happen to you ... well, you'll see.'

Margaret looked towards the entrance. Where were the other guards? Surely they must come? Miguel saw her look, and laughed.

'No hope there, so you might as well give up. I got all four of 'em. Showed myself up the passage so that two of them chased after me; when I'd finished with them, I came back and tackled the other two. They're easy; silly little runts with brains to fit——'

He stopped suddenly, and tiptoed down the passage. Margaret strained her ears, but could hear nothing. Miguel slipped back, and stood flat to the wall, beside the entrance. Outside came an abrupt, high-pitched exclamation. Garm's voice. He must have found the dead guard. Margaret tried to shout a warning; all she achieved was a muffled grunt. It served the opposite of its purpose. Garm came hurrying in. She saw his eyes widen at the sight of her, then Miguel's fist took him on the chin. The blow lifted him clean off his feet, and his head hit the ground a sickening smash.

'Easy,' murmured Miguel. 'Dead easy.'

He crossed back to Margaret, and produced another length of cord to bind her ankles. Despite his contempt for the pygmies, he had decided that it was time to be going. He picked her up and slung her over one shoulder. After a cautious glance up and down the outside passage, he set off in a direction which would, she knew, take them to the disused caverns.

Her eyes opened to meet his. He was sitting a few feet away from her, devouring a slab of mushroom with large, greedy bites.

'Oh, so you've come round, have you?' he said.

She must have fainted as she hung head downwards over his shoulder. She had no recollection of reaching this place. That it was one of the smaller disused caves was obvious to the first glance. For one thing, the liquid in the globes had dulled to a glimmer, for another, it lacked the cleanliness of the inhabited caves. There was the glisten of slime upon the walls, and the floor was littered with accumulated debris and scummy puddles. There was an odour of dampness and the things which grow in stagnant water. She became aware of her surroundings without thought, the whole conscious surface of her mind was taken up with the hurting of her arms. Both hands were numbed to insensibility, but where the tight cord cut into her wrists began an ache which diffused upwards and about her shoulders in a dull throbbing.

The gag had been removed, but her mouth was strained and stiff, moreover it was parched and dry so that her tongue felt hard and useless. When she tried to speak, her voice was little more than a croak. Miguel hesitated a moment, and then decided to push over a bowl of water. By leaning over she could just bring her lips to it.

'My arms,' she said, 'they're hurting so.'

'And why not? If the pygmies had caught me after your lies, I'd have got more than hurt arms.'

Nevertheless, he crossed to her and untied the cords. She brought her arms slowly and painfully forward; returning circulation in her hands was a new agony. Miguel was taking no chances. He waited just long enough for the first numbness to wear off before he rebound her wrists; in front of her this time, and more loosely, though not less securely. Then he went back and resumed his meal.

'Now, we can talk,' he said. 'And I don't care if you yell—they won't find you here.'

Margaret, glancing round the ten yard square cave, could easily believe him. The pygmies had no maps of their caves; they knew them only from familiarity, and when they were no longer needed, they were forgotten. The present pygmy generation would be as lost in these parts as she herself. She did not respond. Miguel went on:

'Thought you'd done with me, didn't you?' And so you damn nearly had. A couple of the little devils almost got me, but I croaked one, and then beat up the other to see what it was all about. Yes, you spun 'em a good yarn—that bit about the cat put paid to my chances—almost. But, by God, your going to be sorry for it.'

He paused, and looked at her. Margaret did her best to stare steadily back. He must not know what a horrible feeling of empty weakness his last vicious threat had caused. He dropped his gaze at last, and grunted.

'Going to be stubborn, eh? It'll be better for you if you're not.'

Still Margaret made no reply. She fought against a rising fear. What did Miguel intend? The very deliberateness of his tone frightened her as much as the threats themselves.

'Now, first, are you going to tell me where this *Sun Bird* is?'

Margaret shook her head.

'No.'

He shrugged his shoulders. 'I thought you'd say that. I'm giving you a chance you don't deserve. Tell me, and there'll be no more trouble.'

She gave no reply.

'A pity,' he said. 'You've got nice hands.'

He put aside his piece of mushroom, and, very deliberately, picked up a flaky lump of rock. With a stone held in his other hand he began to tap it gently and carefully. He went on talking as he worked.

'Do you know what's happening to your friend and his lot down in the prison caves?'

'They're holding out.'

'They *were* holding out, but it won't be long now before the pygmies get them. They're being smoked out. How long will they be able to stay in a cave where they can't see and can't breathe? They've got them by this time, I should guess.' He knocked off a fragment of stone, and laid it carefully on the floor. 'It's too late now,' he persisted, 'you'll never be able to help them. Why can't you be a sensible woman? Tell me where the *Sun Bird* is, and we'll get away together—you'll save a lot of people.'

'No,' said Margaret.

Her heart became heavy. Was Miguel really telling the truth this time? Perhaps, but even so, there might be a chance. After all, the prisoners had beaten off two attacks. She tabulated the alternatives. If it were not true, the position remained as before. If it were, might she not just as well sacrifice the *Sun Bird*? No, there were the other prisoners to be freed. She had got things in the wrong proportion. The handful of fighting men had come to have so much more importance than the hundreds of neutral prisoners, but the latter existed, many women and children among them, so Garm had said. She couldn't sacrifice them all to save herself from Miguel.

He continued to tap methodically. There was now a neat row of little stone flakes on the floor in front of him. She gazed at him, apprehensively wondering what he intended. What was it he had said? That she had nice hands? Well, that was true, but . . .?

'You see,' he was saying conversationally, 'there is no time limit—you will have to tell me sooner or later.'

He laid down his stone and looked at the flakes before him. There were ten of them; little splinters of rock, quite narrow, and no more than an inch and a half long. She wondered . . .?

He picked up one and approached her.

'Come on, now—where is the *Sun Bird*?'

'No,' she said.

'That's your last chance you damned little mule.'

He caught her bound hands in one sinewy fist. With the other he inserted the sharp point of the stone sliver beneath her finger-nail. Then with a quick thrust of his thumb, drove it in.

A streak of vivid pain tore Margaret's arm. She shrieked with the agony of it.

'Will you tell me now?'

Sobbing she shook her head. She could not speak.

'Very well.'

He reached for another slender splinter of stone.

'You've got guts.'

Miguel addressed the quivering, sobbing form on the floor with a kind of reluctant admiration.

Margaret did not hear him. She was struggling in a sea of red agony; clinging fast to one straw of determination —she must not tell—must not tell. . . .

Miguel sat down and looked at her moodily He felt more than a little sick. Why couldn't the fool have told him at first? He didn't want to do this. He had hated her for her betrayal, but that had passed. He'd called her a mule, but, by God, a mule wouldn't have been as stubborn as all that. He had half a mind . . . No, that would be a fool thing to do. When he had gone so far. . . . Anyhow he would try once more. He picked up a stone knife he had filched from one of the dead pygmies, and went back.

Margaret looked up at him standing over her. He was talking. From blurred eyes she could see his mouth moving. She must try to hear what he was saying. The words seemed to come from far away, but she caught their meaning—he was telling her what he proposed to do next. She listened, and her body twitched almost as though it could feel the stone knife. But he talked on, going into details, horrible, sickening. She cried out:

'No, O God, don't do that.'

'Then tell me where the *Sun Bird* is.'

She shook her head. 'I won't.'

'All right then. . . .'

The stone splinter began to descend. Margaret's eyes could not leave it. Why, oh why. . . .? All she had to do was to agree. In another second it would touch, then it would tear, then, O God. . . . It touched. . . .

She screamed: 'I'll tell. . . . I'll tell. . . .'

She twisted aside, sobbing with anguish of spirit. The utter abasement of defeat swept her into a misery beyond any she had known. But if—No, she would have survived one ordeal only to face another—perhaps a worse. Sooner or later she would have broken. . . . But the weakness of prostration was bitter beyond bearing.

Miguel turned away, glad that she could not see his face. He wiped the sweat from his forehead, and flung the stone splinter into a corner. He felt sicker than ever. He could never have done it, he knew that, but the threat had worked, thank God. . . .

He went back to the girl and loosed the cords from her wrists and ankles. From a corner he fetched the clothes he had torn from her, and laid them over her. The tatters of her silk shirt he folded into a pillow for her head. When that was done he crossed the cave and sat down, leaning his back against the wall, listening to the sound of a sobbing so wretched that it seemed interminable.

A revolution was in progress in Miguel's mind. All his anger and hate of her had waned. He could feel nothing but pity for her, and for the things he had had to do. In fact, it was hard to believe that he had done them. It was as though events had conspired, and used him as the tool to hand. The will to live, he supposed Gordon would have called it; the will which was stronger than the form it inhabited. A gust of remorse drove through him. Yet his cunning did not altogether desert him. She must not be allowed to see his regret. She might become stubborn once more; then she would have defeated him indeed. He could not repeat those brutalities. . . .

It was a long time before the abandoned weeping slackened, but, at last, there came into it a more normal note. The first wildness of defeat passed into a calmer hopelessness. Miguel brought a bowl of water, and held it while she drank. She raised her tear-stained face, and fixed her brimming eyes on his own. The expression she saw there surprised her. Through her sobs she murmured:

'Oh, Miguel, why have you hurt me so frightfully?'

Miguel frowned that his remorse should have been visible to her first glance.

'I had to know,' he answered curtly.

'And you'd do it again?'

'If necessary.'

She looked hard at him.

'I don't believe you would.'

'You're going back on it? Because if you are——'

She shuddered. 'No—no. I'll tell you. You've beaten me—broken me. I'll tell you.' She lay back, weeping from sheer weakness, not bothering to hide her face.

Miguel watched the tears. He could not stand this sort of thing much longer.

'Tell me where it is, and I'll go.'

'I can't.'

'You can't?' He raised his hand. 'If you——'

'No. I mean, I can show you the way, but I can't describe it.'

Miguel thought. He should have realised that a description of the way would be impossible. She was right, he must be shown.

'All right, we'll go.'

'And I am coming on the *Sun Bird*.'

He paused at that. 'But——'

'It doesn't matter much if you kill me or not now. I've done all the harm I can—and there might be a chance.'

There would be climbing, Miguel reflected. Alone, he might make it, but if he were encumbered with her, it would be more than doubtful. However, that could wait until the *Sun Bird* was found—it would be easy enough to leave her.

'Put on your clothes,' he said.

Margaret wept again.

'I can't. My hands——'

He was forced to do it for her. He completed the task by

tying the strip of silk over her mouth once more.

'Not taking any risks,' he explained. 'We've got to go through pygmy tunnels. Now, march.'

She took two tottering steps. It was plain he would have to carry her. This time she was not slung across his shoulder, but held in his arms.

Miguel halted at the crux of two, well-lighted passages.

'Which way?' he asked, in an undertone.

Margaret nodded her head to the right. Miguel looked down at her in anger.

'So that's the game, is it? I happen to know that that way leads to Bast's temple. How many times have you played that trick, you damned little snake? I've a good mind to go back with you to the disused caves.'

Margaret's eyes widened with terror and pleading. She shook her head violently, and then nodded in the forward direction.

'All right.' Miguel strode on. 'But if you lead me into a trap, God help you—no one else will.'

They emerged into the fungus cave where she and Mark had first encountered the pygmies. There was not much farther to go now. Margaret resigned herself to helplessness. The luck had run all Miguel's way. They had not encountered a single pygmy to give the alarm, and her pathetically futile plan to lead him into trouble had been detected at its inception. At the back of her mind she knew that he had no intention of taking her with him. Why should he embarrass himself with her? As to what he would do with her, she wondered very little—it did not seem to matter much now.

Miguel started to cross the cave by a beaten path through the fungi. After a few steps he thought better of it, and retraced his way to the wall. Not only would one side thus be safe from attack, but an ambush springing from the fungi must give him a few seconds grace as they crossed the intervening open space. He was becoming uncomfortably suspicious that something unusual was afoot. They had come thus far with never a sign of a pygmy. What could they be up to now? He believed he would have been easier if one or two had put in an appearance. Then he would at least have had the active satisfaction of a fight, and a knowledge of what he was up against, whereas he was feeling distinctly nervous. It had gone too easily. . . .

Part way round the wall, he stopped dead. From somewhere in the big cave had come the murmur of a voice. He looked round, listening and trying to place it. It was not easy, for the rock walls flung echo at echo, and both at original. He could tell no more than that it was in the cave, and growing louder. But, with a shock, he noticed that it was deep and full—no pygmy had ever spoken in such a voice as that. Without hesitation, he made for the great growths. In a well-hidden spot he laid Margaret down, and stood over her, straining his ears.

The sound came nearer. An eerie rumble of speech, still confused into unintelligibility by the echoes. At last, he caught a phrase:

'—And I'm dead certain I'm right this time.'

Miguel could not recognise the distorted voice. The answer made him jump violently.

'Sure, buddy, but you were just as dead certain the other three times, and they were flops.'

Smith's voice. How, in hell's name, had he got here?

'You wait a bit. I know this is the place.'

A muffled cry came from the girl. She had no doubt of Mark's voice. Miguel pounced on her, thrusting one hand fiercely over her mouth, and holding the other clenched in a threatening fist, close to her face.

'What was that?'

'Didn't you hear something? Sounded like a voice.'

'One of them durned pygmies, I guess—let 'em be, unless they ask for trouble, and they've had a bellyfull of that by now. Now, just where is this tunnel of yours? If this ain't the right cave, I'm through. I'm gonna climb one of the blisterin' air shafts.'

'And probably find the water pouring in on you when you get half-way up,' Mark said scathingly. 'I tell you, from where we left the *Sun Bird*, the river runs north, and that means under the mountains. It may be a longer climb when we find a hole, but at least there won't be the water above us.'

'Sure. But how do we know we're gonna find a hole? Seems to me——'

But Miguel waited to hear no more. He had recognised Smith's voice and Ed's; he knew now that the other must be Mark's. How many more there might be in the party he didn't know, and didn't care. The important thing was that they were searching for the *Sun Bird,* and he must get there before they did. He was tempted to leave Margaret where she was, and trust to luck for the rest of the way, but the risk was too big. Instead, he picked her up again, putting her across his shoulders in a less impending fireman's lift, and set off among the fungi.

Miguel had a good sense of direction, and he needed it. Progress between the thick trunks, and over ground littered with twining tendrils was difficult and seemed snail-like, but he managed, at length, to intersect with the middle pathway. Once there, the going became easier, save for the heaviness of the loam underfoot. He hurried on, panting from his own efforts and the weight of the girl. The possibilities of ambush were forgotten; he had only one ambition—to reach the far end of the cave before Smith and his lot. They were not hurrying, and they were taking the longer route by the wall. If he could only get into the opposite tunnel without being seen....

Years of lethargy in the prison caves were not good training for this kind of thing. His lungs laboured painfully; he developed an agonising stitch in his side; sweat trickled down his forehead into his eyes, from his temples into his beard. His breathing seemed loud enough to be heard all over the great cavern. At last, when he had all but despaired of keeping up his speed any longer, the end of the path came into sight.

Behind the last great mushroom trunk, he paused to reconnoitre. The others were not in view, but he could hear their voices not far away. There was the open space to be crossed before he could be safe in the tunnel. If only he could risk leaving the girl ... but it might mean missing the way at the very last. He gathered himself for the effort, and then burst from the growths, sprinting like a hare for the tunnel mouth....

And he made it. No shout followed him. His bare feet had been silent in the soft loam. He had been so sure of detection, that for a moment he failed to realise his luck; then exhilaration poured fresh life into him. He'd beat 'em yet. When they got to the cave it would be just in time to see him drifting away in their precious *Sun Bird*. He'd have the laugh of them in the end. He set off along the passage in a long, swinging stride.

Margaret, slung like an inanimate bundle across his shoulders, wept miserably. She had thought she could weep no more, but a compound of pain, weariness, and disappointment forced out tears of utter wretchedness.... They had been so near; just one word would have done it—if only Miguel had not gagged her. Now the chance was gone. Miguel would take the *Sun Bird*, and leave them all here. Mark, if he ever found her, would despise her for a coward....

'Which way?' Miguel demanded.

She hesitated. He made a threatening move towards her hands. She nodded forward, and he went on. That was the end. There were no more turnings, and she had told the truth when she might have misled him. But if she had.... O God, hadn't she been hurt enough already?

One more effort. She must make one last attempt. She raised her free hand to the gag. The touch of the soft silk felt like knives in her injured fingers. But she must do it. She clenched her teeth so that her jaw ached. The bleeding fingers fumbled at the silk....

CHAPTER VI

'THIS,' said Mark, pointing to the tunnel mouth, 'is it.'

The rest of the party was not impressed. Smith yawned elaborately. The burly Ed grunted. Even Zickle would appear to have lost faith. Gordon was alone in that he did not look sceptical—but neither did he look enthusiastic.

Mark walked forward and examined the walls just within the entrance. He pointed with excitement to a scar on the stone.

'It is,' he cried. 'Look here.' The others came round him.

'Isn't that a bullet mark?' he demanded.

Smith peered closely.

'You've said it,' he admitted. 'But what of it?'

'Don't you see? This is where the fight was—one of my bullets did that.'

The attitude of the others underwent a slight change; so slight that it was hard to rate it higher than a faint diminution of disbelief.

'Well, I'll believe it when I see your *Sun Bird*,' said Smith, expressing a good average of the general feeling. 'The Lord knows how long we've been looking for it, but it feels to me like a week, and I'm beginning to think it just don't exist no more.'

'Come on,' Mark said, leading the way up the tunnel, 'how much'll you bet?'

'Nothin', buddy. I never steal toys from kids.'

'It's lucky for you——' He broke off.

Somewhere ahead a voice was shouting. The words were indistinguishable, and broke off abruptly. A moment later came a piercing scream.

'What the hell——?'

'Pygmy,' said Ed briefly.

'Pygmy, my foot. That was a woman. C'm on.'

Smith charged ahead; the rest followed in a bunch. They rounded the corner and came to the crossways.

'Which?' Smith called back over his shoulder.

'Straight on,' panted Mark.

A long stretch of straight, another corner, and then they found her; a bundle of torn dishevelment, whimpering pitifully. She raised her tear-stained face as they came.

'Margaret,' cried Mark.

Smith stopped short beside her.

'Great God, look at her hands!'

'Miguel. Stop him. He'll get the *Sun Bird*,' she moaned.

Smith charged on, leaving her to be attended by Mark, but this time he was not the leader. Zickle had sped ahead; there was an old score to be settled between him and Miguel. He was a better runner than Smith, and drew off rapidly. Ed pounded up alongside Smith, and the two began to slack off.

'Let Zickle have his fun,' he puffed. 'And if he don't settle him, we'll be right there to finish it.' He drew his improvised club from his belt.

On ahead, Zickle had rounded the last corner. There

was nothing now between him and the opening into the flooded cave—nor was there any sign of Miguel. He left the passage, and came out on the top of the ramp.

At the foot of it lay a craft like a huge, silver eggshell; a ragged figure was fumbling desperately at the line which moored it. With a shout, the Negro turned and charged down the slope.

Miguel gave a startled glance, and leapt aboard. He staggered a moment on the slippery roof, and then bent down, trying to loosen the mooring line from that end. It was stubborn. Zickle sped on, taking a flying leap at the *Sun Bird*. Miguel straightened to meet him. As the Negro's feet touched the roof, Miguel's fist met his jaw. It was a good punch, but it could not check the impetus of the leap. Zickle's head went back, but his feet slipped forward, knocking Miguel's legs from beneath him, and the two rolled on the curving roof together.

Miguel took his chance for a hold while the other was still dazed. Zickle rallied in time to break it before it could be well established, and tried for one of his own. Miguel brought his knee into action. Simultaneously, he got his fingers on the other's nostrils, and the mill was well in action. If there was a nasty trick which Miguel did not know, it was not his fault; if, in Zickle's native village, the rules of wrestling were unknown, who should blame him?

Smith and Ed reached the top of the ramp, and stood looking down on the two squirming figures—it was an inelegant sight.

'Hell, he's a filthy scrapper,' said Smith.

'Well, Zickle ain't no pansy, neither. Just you watch the boy.'

The Negro had fixed a scissor hold, crushing Miguel like a vice. The great black thighs were tensed hard as stone. They could hear Miguel gasp with the pressure as he tried to keep groping black hands from his eyes. He made a desperate attempt to break the scissor, and failed. The black seized his advantage, and his hands were on the other's face. Miguel screamed, twisting wildly. The interlocked bodies slipped, hung a moment, and then slithered down the curved hull into the water.

For some seconds little could be seen but a seething and

splashing. When they again became visible the hold had been broken, and both were threshing wildly in attempts to find a grip. With Miguel's hand on the Negro's throat, they sank again. For long seconds there was no sign, then a single head reappeared. Miguel's.

'Well, I'll be——'

But even as Smith spoke, Zickle's woolly head bobbed into view behind the other. Black arms reached forward; black fingers clenched deep, like talons, into Miguel's neck, and the two sank once more.

The watchers stood intent for a long time.

A few bubbles troubled the surface....

CHAPTER VII

MARGARET regained consciousness in a leisurely manner. She seemed to drift from sleep into the comatose, and thence into an awareness of her surroundings. Thus it was with no shock of surprise that she found herself in the cabin of the *Sun Bird*.

Nevertheless, the full implication did not come home for some minutes. When it did, it was in a flood of thanksgiving which completely swept away the earlier misery of her defeat. It had been worth it—worth all the agony. The victory was hers after all. Had she given in only half an hour earlier, Miguel would have won. He would have got through the caves unmolested, and now be floating down the subterranean river. No other tonic could have acted with the power of that realisation—the sense of triumph flowed in like a surge of new strength.

But it was not physical strength. Her muscles remained heavy and slack; it was an exertion to lift one arm. When she did raise it, she found that the hand was wrapped in a thick bundle of bandages. She tried the other hand, and found that it had been similarly treated. Feeling utterly helpless, she called out in a voice which surprised her by its weakness. There was a scraping on the roof; presently Mark swung himself in through the open door. He bent over her.

'Better, darling?'

She smiled up at him, and tilted her head farther back. He kissed her lips.

'Ever so much. What's happened?'

'Never mind about that now. Just lie quiet. I'll get you some food.'

'I couldn't eat it, but I'd like a drink.'

'What sort? Tea?'

'Tea? Did you say tea?'

Mark laughed. 'Yes, tea. We're almost civilised again. You can have tea or cocoa, but there's no brandy left.'

'Tea,' Margaret chose firmly. 'You know,' she added, 'I never really thought I'd ever drink tea again.'

'Soon you'll be able to have all the tea in the world—we're going to get out of this.' Mark started up a small electric stove, and rummaged in a cupboard for the tea-caddy as he talked. 'Just as soon as the others come back, we're going to cast off and slide away down the river.'

'The others?' she said. 'Who are they?'

'There's Smith who is tough, but has brains as well. He's American. There's Ed who is tougher and more American. And Gordon who is English, in spite of his name. He's an archaeologist. Just the three of 'em. There were more.'

'I heard that there were over a hundred of you.'

'Oh yes. What I meant was that our party was bigger. We had Zickle, the nigger, and Mahmud, who was some kind of Arab.'

'What happened to them?'

Mark hesitated.

'You ought to rest, you know.'

'Nonsense, Mark. I've been asleep for Heaven knows how long. I want to know what's happened. I don't understand it at all. You and the rest are supposed to be in the prison caves—not only in them, but besieged there—instead, you're wandering about here. And all the way with Miguel I didn't see a single pygmy. Tell me all about it while I drink the tea.'

Mark gave an account of the pygmy attacks, and their defeat.

'But didn't they try to smoke you out? Miguel said something——'

'Yes, that was their last move. They'd have brought it off, too, if the water hadn't come in.'
'Where from?'
'From the tunnel our people had been making. They must have got through just in time.'
'What happened to them?'
'I don't know.'
'But weren't they washed down?'
'We didn't see them. I expect they got jammed in there, poor devils.'
'What happened when the water came into your cave?'
'Luckily it couldn't come at a great rate, the tunnel was too small for that, so we had plenty of time to get ready.'
He went on to tell of the building of rafts from mushroom trunks. Margaret interrupted again:
'But what had happened to the pygmies?'
'Oh, they'd gone. One look at the water was enough for them—and we weren't far behind them. It wasn't very difficult to get along. The water really rose quite slowly—particularly when it had to flood the larger caves. What worried me most was that I couldn't remember whether it was a gradual rise all the way to the prison caves entrance. If so, we should be all right, but if there was a dip, or more than one dip on the way, we'd probably get trapped. But I needn't have worried, for there were no dips worth troubling about. The other worry was lest the pygmies might trap us. You know what they do when there's a break—knock in the passage at a strategic point, and sacrifice all the part that's beyond it. If they did that and we were on the wrong side of the fall, it would be all up.
'Luckily they didn't. We just kept on pushing the rafts ahead and making better time than the water. Once or twice we even had to wait until the water rose enough to float the front raft before we could get along. It was as simple as could be. We never got a glimpse of a pygmy or a "native" or anyone else the whole way. In fact, it was too good to last. The balloon went up when we reached the last big cave.
'Of course you've never seen that particular cave. It's one of the biggest in the whole place, I should think. At one end is the passage through which we came, and at the

other is the only connection between that system and this. And it's a narrow connection, too. Quite a small passage, and before you can get at it, you've got to reach a ledge a hundred feet up the bare wall. Well, I hadn't thought a great deal on what we should do when we got there. I'd got a rough idea that we'd just sit on our rafts while the water rose and floated them up to the ledge, and I hadn't reckoned at all with what else we might find.

'We came in to discover one of the nastiest shemozzles I've ever seen in full swing. Every living soul in the prison caves had rushed there at the first alarm; the pygmies, the prisoners themselves, and the "natives", too, and the whole lot had arrived at just about the same time. On the ledge was a crowd of pygmies dangling ropes to haul their pals up, but everybody else wanted those ropes, too. Some of the prisoners were trying to climb up, and the little devils at the top were jerking to shake them off. The pygmies down below were hardly having a look in. Everybody else was dead sure that if anybody was going to be saved, it wouldn't be pygmies, and the little chaps were coming in for a rough time. But those up on top were just as sure that they weren't going to save prisoners while pygmies were left to drown. They succeeded in dislodging most of the climbers so that they fell on those below. If they couldn't get rid of them that way, they just cut the ropes and let 'em drop. Everyone that dropped from fifty or sixty feet laid out four or five of the scrappers below. So far as I could see, not a single prisoner had reached the top yet, and it didn't look as if any would.

'Already the water was ankle-deep at the base of the wall, and everyone there was pretty nearly mad with fright. I don't blame them—it's not a nice lookout when you know the water's going to rise and trap you. And swimming—which only a few of the prisoners and none of the pygmies knew—wouldn't help them. Those who could swim might have a little longer to wait for the end, that was all. As it was, the whole lot had lost their heads, and were hitting out wildly in a blind panic. And in the middle of it all we came out of the passage, shoving our rafts.

'It was a minute or two before anybody noticed us, but when they did—well, it beats description. They just forgot about their own scrapping, and came for us. We didn't stand a chance. There were only a few of us, and hundreds of them, wild with fright. There were fists and stones and a few knives, and the women raked with hands like claws. They'd have had our eyes out in a couple of minutes. Smith yelled to us to get back. Most of us did, but a few stuck to their rafts and tried to defend them—I don't know what happened to them. We saw them go down in the rush, and that was all.

'Then, of course, another scrap started. There wasn't a tenth the number of rafts necessary to carry them all, and they started in to settle who was going to be saved, and who was going to drown. It was a nastier fight than I ever want to see again. The water down our end of the cave was waist-deep now and the prime tactic of the day seemed to be to thrust an opponent under and stand on him or her while one clutched firmly to the raft with one hand and defended the position with the other. The screeching and shouting in most of the languages of Africa and Europe was ear-splitting. We stood back with Smith and watched.

'What his plan was, I don't know. I thought at the time that he intended to let the rest put one another out of action before he charged in to recover some, at least, of the rafts. Even two would be enough for our particular party, for a couple of mushroom trunks would support a considerable number provided that they were content to cling to the sides instead of climbing on top. Possibly that was his idea; anyhow, we stood and watched with our backs to the tunnel through which we had just come. I was beginning to wonder whether it wasn't about time to take a hand when I got a nudge in the back. I looked round to find a big mushroom trunk which had drifted gently out of the tunnel on the rising stream.

'We needn't have made those rafts at all. The way we had come was simply full of floating logs and puff-balls. Whether they were the scattered remains of our rampart, or of fungi newly broken off by the water, I don't know, but, wherever they came from, there were plenty of them. The fighting round the rafts stopped almost at once, and there was a rush at the flotsam. Soon, there was more than enough rubbish drifting in to support the lot of us.

'Our small group got hold of three trunks, and by the time we had managed to get a couple of ropes round them and scramble on top, the water was up to our armpits.

'Up the other end of the cave, the pygmies on the ledge were working furiously to save such of their pals as were still standing. Little white figures went swinging and bumping up the perpendicular face to the top. Then the ropes were untied, and thrown down for another load. They were working mighty quickly against time, but time looked like winning. Already, even at that shallower end, the water was waist-high on the pygmies, and there were still scores of them to be hauled up. Most of them were scared stiff or practically screaming with fright and hitting at the water as if they could push it away. Poor little devils—most of them had never seen more water than there is in a drinking bowl or a small stream, until the breaks started.

'We began to paddle over with our hands, taking as much floating rubbish with us as we could. After all, you can't sit by and watch even pygmies drown like that; you forget you've been fighting them an hour or two before.

'Then it was just a matter of waiting while the water rose and gradually lifted the lot of us towards the ledge. The pygmies up above craned over and looked at us, and held long discussions. It was pretty clear what they were talking about. If they were to close the tunnel leading to the outer caves, they would not only seal the break, but finish with us as well: on the other hand, all the pygmies (and there were plenty of them) floating about with us would have to be sacrificed. They were faced with the nasty point of whether it was worth it. Eventually, they decided it was not. Not so much, I think, from humanitarianism as from a fatalistic sense of defeat. I don't think they had much feeling of gratitude towards us for saving their pals—though that may be an injustice; but the idea that the pygmy world is doomed, and that they can do nothing so save it, has been growing of late, and, with it, the notion that whatever they do doesn't matter a great deal.

'Anyhow, whatever the reason, they waited until we were about half-way up, and began shouting down to those with us; then they went away. Mahmud explained that the suggestion was that we should all get out together, and that the pygmies with us should stay and close the passage behind them in order to confine the water to the prison system.

'And, to cut it short, that's what happened. We gave them a hand; the minute the tunnel was closed, they scampered off, and Mahmud with them. We've scarcely seen one of them since. I think they've gone north to the highest levels. Mahmud didn't think much of the *Sun Bird* idea, and held that the safest course was to keep with them. The rest of the prisoners scattered in groups, looking for ways out. We stuck together, trying to find the old *Sun Bird*; it seemed the best bet.'

'And when you'd found her?' Margaret asked.

'The others were going downstream to find a way out.'

'Not you?'

'There was still something in the caves that I wanted more than my liberty—I was going to look for it.'

She smiled up at him.

'Darling.'

After the interlude, she said, with a frown:

'But Miguel—what happened to him?'

He gave Smith's account of the fight. She shuddered.

'Poor Miguel.'

'What?' Mark exclaimed, looking down at the bandages on her hands. 'After that?'

'He was weak. He almost cried as he did it. Perhaps in different circumstances . . .'

Mark stared speechlessly.

'I don't understand,' he managed at last.

'Never mind, dear, I didn't expect it. Tell me what's happened to the others. Didn't you say there were three of them?'

'They've gone to cut up some mushrooms—there's not much food aboard for five. They ought to be back soon.'

Mounted upon the *Sun Bird*'s instrument board was an electric clock. With the discovery that it was still going, the passage of time became suddenly more important. The recent mental habits became superseded by the old outlook. The clock stood for change and progress, its moving hands were a constant reminder of time wasted, things to be done, and, more uncomfortably, things that now never could be done. Margaret stared at it with fascination and dislike. There had been points in favour of the timeless existence once one got used to it. To see the hands sliding irrevocably over the numbers, brushing them into the past, depressed her. There was much to be said for a permanent today which had no finished, inflexible yesterdays....

The hands had covered an hour before a hail called Mark from the cabin. She heard him shout an answering greeting, and felt the *Sun Bird* manoeuvred until her door was against the ramp. Mark came back with two tattered men, bearded like himself. Their large size crowded the little cabin.

'Smith and Ed,' he introduced. 'Where's Gordon?'

'Comin' along right behind us,' said Smith.

He inquired how Margaret was feeling now, and made uncomplimentary references to Miguel.

'Say, I'm almost sorry Zickle got him. I'd have liked to show him where he got off, myself.'

'It'll soon be all right,' she assured him. 'It might have been worse.' She thought with a shudder of the thin stone knife.

Smith looked down at her and shrugged his shoulders.

'That must be the Christian spirit they used to tell me about at school. By God, if a guy had done tricks like that to me——' He left the sentence unfinished, and turned to Mark. 'We'd best get the stuff aboard—no good wastin' time.'

The other two went outside and started to hand in slabs of mushroom head which Smith stowed carefully in the stern.

Gordon came down the slope just as they were finishing. He held one hand behind his back; the other was empty. Beside him stalked a rusty-looking cat.

'Where've you been?' Mark demanded. 'We were beginning to think you'd got yourself into trouble—and, anyhow, you were supposed to be fetching mushrooms. Where are they?'

Gordon shook his head.

'I forgot them,' he admitted. 'But look what I did get.'

He brought the hand from behind his back and held

out a shining globe, somewhat smaller than those which glowed in the cavern roof. The others came round him.

'It took some time to get it off,' he explained.

The cat left his side, and prowled towards the door of the *Sun Bird*. It disappeared within.

'But what's the idea?' Smith asked. 'We've got electric light, and the batteries are not down yet, not by a long way.'

Gordon regarded him pityingly.

'You poor mutt,' he said, slipping for once into the alien tongue. 'Don't you see what we've got? Cold light, man. No waste by heat, no power supply necessary, depreciation scarcely noticeable. It'll mean millions for all of us. Why, there's nothing we couldn't get for it, once we've analysed the stuff inside. Cold light; it's been the dream of the world, like—like the universal solvent—and we've got it.'

Smith grunted.

'Maybe you right, but we ain't out of this yet. Come on. Stow it aboard. We've got enough mushrooms, anyway.'

They crammed into the little cabin. A gingery bundle of fur had curled itself up on Margaret's lap.

'Look,' she said. 'Bast's come back. Where did you find her?'

'Bast? Oh, that cat. I don't know. It came sniffing around while I was getting the lamp. When I came back, it came too.'

'I thought she was dead, poor thing.'

'You can't kill 'em,' said Smith. 'African cats are made that way. Now, stow that light some place, Gordon, and we'll get goin'.'

He climbed to the roof, while Ed stepped on to the ramp, and loosed the moorings.

'O.K.?'

'O.K.'

Ed gave a mighty heave, and scrambled aboard.

The *Sun Bird* slid out upon the cavern lake. Towards the middle she swung a little in the gentle current. She turned, drifting slowly towards the black hole in the wall. The beam of the searchlight sprang ahead. The sides of the passage closed upon her. The blue-white lamps of the cavern fell behind.

CHAPTER VIII

'LIGHT ahead.' Smith's voice came echoing back to the rest.

Almost too good to be true. So many hours of climbing through natural tunnels, narrow clefts, booming caves, and up all but impossible 'chimneys' had wearied them almost to hopelessness. Had it not been for the doggedness of the two Americans they would have given up long ago, and stayed to die in some corner of the labyrinth. It was chiefly Ed's amazing strength which had brought them so far, for it was he who, by bracing back against one side, and hands and feet against the other, had managed to scale the perpendicular 'chimneys', and throw down a rope to the rest.

How long it was since they had left the *Sun Bird* rocking on the underground river, and started the climb, none of them knew. Two or three days, perhaps, but it had seemed a short lifetime. There had been disappointments, dead-ends, retracing of steps and fresh starts. They had been confronted with cracks too narrow for passage, walls too smooth to be climbed, caves from which the only outlet was a split in the roof. Margaret, still weak at the start, had soon become exhausted. Mark had helped her until his strength gave out and Ed came to the rescue. The calm patience of the two Americans amazed them. Again and again they turned back from dead-ends without bitterness or the futility of anger, and sought another route. If they felt any despondency, not a trace of it was allowed to show, and their confidence buoyed up the rest.

Except when Ed performed his prodigies of climbing, Smith was in the lead. The *Sun Bird*'s searchlight was hung against his chest, and a battery mounted on his back; next came Ed, carrying Margaret, then Gordon, adding to the illumination with his globe, while Mark, with another lamp and a smaller battery, brought up the rear. Each had started with a pack of food in the form of mushroom slabs, but these had now dwindled to a quarter of their original size, and what remained was dry and leathery.

Smith's call put fresh life into them all. Mark forgot that his feet, on which the boots were coming to pieces, were swollen with great blisters, and hurried on till he was close behind Gordon.

'Daylight?' he called.

'Sure, sunlight,' shouted Smith.

They emerged from a crevice on to a narrow ledge. The sun was about to set behind a line of rugged mountains. It was some time before anyone spoke.

'Gees,' said Ed, at last, as he lowered Margaret, 'ain't that just glorious? There ain't no sweller sight in the whole of God's world—an' I reckoned I wasn't never gonna see it no more. Yeh, we've sure been missing somethin' down there.'

Mark crossed to Margaret. He put his arm round her.

'You mustn't cry, darling. It's all over now.'

'I know,' she managed. 'That's why I'm crying. It's so lovely and I'm so glad. Oh, Mark....' She lifted her bandaged hands and put her arms about his neck.

Gordon laid his light globe down carefully and turned to observe the sunset with the air of one witnessing an interesting, and slightly unusual phenomenon.

'Well, what do we do now?' he asked in a practical tone as the last arc sank from view.

'Sleep,' Smith told him promptly.

'You've said it,' Ed agreed.

'What we got to do is get goin' as soon as maybe,' Smith observed through a mouthful of shrivelled and unappetising mushroom. 'There ain't no tellin' when the next break'll come, nor how big it's goin' to be. If we aim to get the rest out, we've got to move right now. Here's my idea.' He turned to Gordon. 'You speak a bit of Arabic, don't you?' Gordon nodded. 'Well, you and Mark get along to the nearest village, find out where we are, and get hold of something to ride—don't matter what, camels, horses, mules—and get some of those Arab duds, burnouses, or whatever they call 'em, for Ed an' me. We three wait here for you, and then we all cut off together for civilisation. How's that?'

Gordon demurred.

'Why don't you go? You're both about twice our size, and size tells with Arabs.'

'Two good reasons. One is that we only know about two words of the lingo, but you know it well, and Mark's got money which is a good substitute for lingo any place. And the other is these duds.' He indicated the shreds of his uniform. 'We'd run into a *goumier* like as not, and that'd be that.'

'What's a *goumier*?' Margaret asked.

'Kinda native cop they run to in these parts. He gets twenty-five francs if he brings in a Legion deserter, dead or alive—and a dead man's less trouble.'

'But you aren't deserters.'

'No, but who's goin' to believe that till they know about the pygmies? It's no fun bein' found innocent if you've been bumped off first. What's more, it seems to me we're goin' to save a hell of a lot of trouble and argument if we desert right now. What say?' He looked questioningly at Ed.

'Suits me.'

'And after that?' Mark asked.

'We make for some place where we can get white man's pants. Then, when we're all swell and classy, we spill the beans about the pygmies—and, believe me, we'll have to do a mighty lot of persuading.'

'But we've got proof,' Gordon pointed to his globe.

'An' we'll need it. Well, what about my proposition? You guys willin'?'

'Yes,' Mark agreed, 'but where are we going to find a village?'

Smith looked down from the ledge into the rocky valley. He pointed to a small, muddy stream which meandered along the dusty bottom.

'See that? I'm willin' to bet it's someone's water supply. They like it that way round here. Just you follow downstream, and you'll find a village pretty soon.'

'Right you are. So long, and look after Margaret.'

'And look after the lamp,' added Gordon. 'Don't let that damned cat get anywhere near it.'

The three left on the ledge watched them climb down and turn to the north.

'They won't be in danger? You're sure?' Margaret asked Ed.

'Betcha life,' he replied with an assurance which sounded more nearly absolute than he expected.

A week later a party which had come into Algiers the previous day by the line from Jelfa, sat round a café table. They attracted a certain amount of unwelcome interest by their curious appearance. For one thing, they were accompanied by a desert cat of unattractive, even repulsive, aspect; for another, the girl's hands were heavily wrapped in bandages, but most remarkable was the complexion of one of her three male companions. The forehead and the upper part of his face was badly sunburned to a vivid, angry red, while the rest was of a startling white, as though a beard might recently have been removed. He addressed the other two, who wore beards neatly trimmed and pointed.

'I wish to Heaven I'd had the sense to keep on my beard. I feel like a circus clown.'

Margaret laughed.

'Never mind, dear, I like you better without it—and your face will soon even up.'

Smith knocked back his fourth brandy that morning with great appreciation.

'That's what I call a white man's drink.' He ordered another, and looked up the street.

'Where the hell's Gordon? You ought to be gettin' along.'

'He's gone to get a case for that precious globe of his—he said it might take him half an hour or so.'

'Well, he's late already.' Smith paused, and a worried frown came over his face. 'You're sure you've got this right?' he said. 'You three go and lay the information, but you don't say anything about Ed an' me. We're the absolute last shot in the locker. If you can't convince 'em any other way at all, you can bring us into it, an' we'll try.'

'I don't see what they could do even if they found out who you are,' said Margaret. 'After all, the term of service in the Legion is only five years, and that's up long ago.'

'If they chalked us up as deserters it ain't over, you betcha sweet life,' Ed replied. 'Not by a million miles.

And they're just crazy over deserters.'

'There he is,' said Mark suddenly.

Gordon was hurrying along the crowded footpath towards them. He looked hot, moreover, his face suffered from the same varie-colouring as afflicted Mark's. In one hand he clutched a clumsy, cubical leather box, and in the other, a newspaper which he waved at them.

'What's the rush?' Smith inquired, as he came up to the table. 'Seein' you're a half-hour late right now, why bother?'

'Look at this,' Gordon panted, throwing the paper on to the table, and dropping into a chair.

'Good God!' Mark had caught sight of a headline.

The four craned over to read:

MYSTERY OF THE NEW SEA

and underneath, a lesser caption:

LEVEL SINKS 24 CMS. IN ONE NIGHT

'What's that?' said Ed.

' 'Bout nine or ten inches,' muttered Mark, reading ahead.

> 'The New Sea, which has on several occasions failed to show the expected rate of progress, sprang a new surprise on the experts last night. The engineers in charge of the work were hurriedly summoned from their beds soon after retiring for the night. Upon arrival at the observation station they quickly discovered that the level of the New Sea was dropping rapidly. "It was amazing," said M. Radier, who is in command of the Qabés works, when interviewed by our correspondent. "We have never experienced anything like it before. The level continued to show its usual rise until ten o'clock, and then began to fall. The men left in charge became alarmed, and summoned us to the scene. We at once verified their observations with the gravest concern. The fall continued throughout the night although all the pumps are at work as usual. This morning it had dropped by 23·832 centimetres, at

which figure it remains. It is a very serious thing for us, meaning as it does, a loss of many weeks of work." Asked if he could offer any reason, M. Radier replied: "No. It is inexplicable." At the suggestion that the same thing might happen again, he shrugged his shoulders. "It is impossible to say until we know more," he declared.

'Another responsible official, M. Pont, when interviewed, replied: "The fall must have been caused by a sudden subsidence of the sea bottom." Asked if this was usual, he said: "No, but it does not surprise me. The earth is as full of holes as a sponge." Our interviewer then suggested that so great a volume of water might cause danger, should it reach the internal fires. M. Pont smiled as he replied: "You need have no fear of that; if it had reached the internal fires, I should not be talking to you now." '

There was a great deal more, chiefly repetitive. The four read it through, and looked up at one another. Smith took a drink of brandy, and lit a cigarette with care.

'Poor devils,' he said. 'I guess that's that.'

Mark nodded. Ten inches of water over that vast area represented an unthinkable number of gallons. Yes, it was the end. The big break had come. There would be no rescues from the pygmy caves now.

'I wonder if any of them got out?' Margaret said.

A few, Gordon thought, probably quite a number of the prisoners had been lucky enough to climb shafts here and there, but the pygmies, no. . . .

'Well,' said Ed, and there was a note of relief in his voice. 'That lets us out. There's no good spinnin' the yarn now, and I don't mind tellin' you folks that I'm gonna be a lot easier in the mind when I'm out of French territory.'

'Me, too,' Smith agreed, 'but where are we goin'?'

'London, of course,' said Gordon. 'Do you mean to tell me that you've forgotten that you are to be members of the board of the Cold Light Company Limited?'

Margaret looked round the group.

'Yes. London,' she agreed. 'But there's something much more important than the Cold Light Company. You're going to attend a wedding.'

Smith tossed down the last of his brandy.
'Free drinks?' he inquired.
'Oceans of them.'
He rose, and dragged Ed with him.
'Good news, sister. Lead us to London.'